Mystery from History

Mystery from History

Dayle Campbell Gaetz

*Dayle Campbell
Gaetz*

Orca Book Publishers

Canadian Cataloguing in Publication Data
Gaetz, Dayle, 1947–
Mystery from history

ISBN 1-55143-200-5

I. Title.
PS8563.A25317M93 2001   jC813'.54   C2001-910133-3
PZ7.G1185My 2001

First published in the United States, 2001

Library of Congress Catalog Card Number: 2001086680

Orca Book Publishers gratefully acknowledges the support for our
publishing programs provided by the following agencies: The Govern-
ment of Canada through the Book Publishing Industry Development
Program (BPIDP), The Canada Council for the Arts, and the British
Columbia Arts Council.

Cover illustration by Ljuba Levstek
Interior illustrations by Cindy Ghent
Cover design by Christine Toller
Printed and bound in Canada

IN CANADA:
Orca Book Publishers
PO Box 5626, Station B
Victoria, BC Canada
V8R 6S4

IN THE UNITED STATES:
Orca Book Publishers
PO Box 468
Custer, WA USA
98240-0468

03 02 01 • 5 4 3 2 1

To Elaine, Margo, and Karen
for their friendship
and active imaginations.

... Acknowledgements ...

With thanks to Bob Tyrrell and Andrew Wooldridge at Orca Book Publishers for their help and excellent suggestions as I worked to complete this manuscript.

... one ...

The House

Katie raced down the steep hill as fast as she dared, bouncing through potholes that rattled her teeth, standing on her bike pedals to keep from bumping too hard against the seat. Rotten Road, she and her friends called this narrow, winding road, because it really was. Katie gritted her teeth. Her eyes half closed in the wind, she could barely see. She was going so fast! This time she would beat Sheila for sure.

Almost at the bottom she glanced up, confident she would be there first.

For that first split second the shock was too much to hide; her mouth dropped open, her eyes bugged out. Sheila was standing where the ground leveled off, waiting, leaning casually against her bike. Sheila yawned and glanced at her watch as if she had been waiting for hours.

Katie bit back a quick burst of anger, pushed away a dark curl that escaped her helmet, and braked to a stop beside her friend. Second. Again.

They were almost the same age, but even at that Sheila managed to come first. She had turned twelve last week and Katie's birthday was still two weeks away. Sheila was a little taller and a lot more athletic, and she always moved with an easy grace that reminded Katie of a cat.

Sheila had the most interesting face in the world. Not pale with embarrassing pink cheeks like Katie's face. No. Sheila's skin was brown and white, decorated with so many lovely freckles that Katie sometimes wondered if it was really white with brown freckles or brown with white freckles. Either way, Katie envied her.

A loud cry made them both look back up Rotten Road. Rusty bounced around the bend at top speed with both legs waving frantically in the air. His mouth formed a perfectly round hole in his face, his straight red hair stood on end in front of his helmet, and his own scream chased him down the hill.

Out of control, Rusty headed straight for Sheila and Katie. Katie jumped to the right, Sheila leapt to the left, and Rusty barreled between them, his mouth still open, although the scream had died. With Sheila and Katie out of the way, he could now see the mud puddle stretched out in front of him like a small brown lake. He slammed on his brakes. Or, at least, his front brake. The bike stopped, the back end flipped up, and Rusty catapulted into the air. For a moment the two girls watched him fly, arms outstretched, legs kicking wildly as though he could run through the air. He landed smack in the center of the puddle and disappeared in a spray of brown water.

No one moved. Katie stared at the bike; the back wheel still spun crazily, round and round. She looked at her cousin, lying face down in the water. She was about to wade in and help him when Rusty lifted his head, sputtered, and spat out a mouthful of muddy water. His face looked as if it had been dipped in chocolate milk. His eyes opened, two blue circles in the brown. "The first one to laugh is dead," he announced.

Katie glanced at Sheila. Her friend's lips were pressed hard together, her eyes crinkled with laughter. Katie bit her lip, looked quickly away and found herself facing the old mansion. Any thought of laughter died. She had never been so close to the old house before.

It brooded above them like a giant about to awake. The smell of it filled the air, a smell of evil and decay. Huge water stains made irregular patterns on the rust-colored paint, and in many places the paint had worn completely off, exposing the gray, weathered boards beneath. Dozens of tiny windows stared down ominously, like sinister eyes behind dark glasses. Amazingly, not one of them was broken. The house seemed to be waiting for them, daring them to come closer.

Katie couldn't resist the challenge. "Let's go inside!" she said.

"Are you kidding?" Rusty pushed himself up and sloshed out of the puddle. He was less than a year younger than Katie, but small for his age, and the clumsiest person she had met in her entire life. He wiped a drip of water from his chin. His shirt and pants were plastered with thick mud. When he put his head back to look up at Katie, water trickled from his red hair. "I agreed to come down here. I never said anything about going inside. Besides, the stories …"

"If you're going to tell us about the moving lights and weird sounds again, don't bother," Katie interrupted. "I don't believe any of it. Those old stories don't mean anything."

Katie would never admit it to her cousin, but it was those very stories that made her want to explore the deserted house. For years now people had reported seeing lights and hearing sounds there. Some even insisted it was haunted. This deserted, isolated house so close to the city had always intrigued her. Katie might not believe in ghosts, but she couldn't resist a good mystery. Even though she had no idea why Sheila and Rusty had finally agreed to come down here with her, she wasn't about to argue. Katie pushed her bike quickly toward the house, hoping the other two would follow.

An old wooden gate hung by one hinge from a rotting fence post. There was no sign of a fence, but bushes grew thickly on either side of the gate. A path, almost hidden by weeds and long grass, led to the stairs.

Katie was not surprised when Rusty whispered, "I'll stay here and guard the bikes." Her cousin had too much imagination for his own good and usually managed to frighten himself with his own thoughts.

If he didn't want to come that was fine with Katie. If

it were up to her, Rusty wouldn't be tagging along with them anyway. But her mom had to be such a nice aunt and volunteer to babysit him when his mother had to work. So, guess who got stuck with him all day?

Katie propped her bike against a blackberry bush and slipped off her helmet and knapsack. "Come on, Sheila," she said.

A feeling of dread settled over her the minute she set foot on the path, a strange sort of tingling, as if someone was watching her every step. In spite of this, or maybe because of it, she couldn't bring herself to look up at the windows. She stopped and waited for Sheila to catch up. Side by side, not quite touching, they crept toward the wide, wooden stairway. On each side of it were crumbling, once-white balustrades. At the bottom, Katie glanced over her shoulder. Rusty rested one foot on the high pedal of his bike, pointed toward Rotten Road, poised for instant flight.

Katie and Sheila started up the stairs together, soft-footed as cats. On the top step they stopped to study the wide, wooden verandah. Deep gouges were cut into the old wood and snaked toward the front door. Running alongside the gouges were long, black smudges that looked fresh and new. Katie reached sideways to grab Sheila's arm. Her fingers waved in empty air. She whirled around.

Halfway down the stairs Sheila stood with one foot on a lower step, ready to run. The top half of her body twisted back toward Katie, round blue eyes fixed on

Katie's face. Sheila's mouth opened slightly, as if ready to yell for help; her shoulder-length hair, the same light brown as her freckles, flew out from her face.

"Chicken!" Katie mouthed, and motioned her to come up. But Sheila shook her head stubbornly. Her eyebrows were set in that obstinate line Katie knew too well, her head tilted back so that her chin jutted toward Katie as if daring her to find fault. Katie frowned and turned away.

After so many months of wanting to explore the house, Katie refused to give up now that she had finally convinced Sheila to come so close. She studied the wide, wooden door. On both sides and above it were panels of intricately decorated stained glass. Her eyes wandered lightly over the patterns until they came to rest on a small section of clear glass, exactly the right height for peeking through. It was oval shaped, just like an eye.

She raised one foot onto the verandah, paused, swallowed and told herself it was now or never. Quickly, before she could change her mind, Katie forced her feet across the verandah to the door. She stopped. There, on the threshold, were more black smudges and deep gouges that cut into good, unweathered wood. Something very heavy had been dragged through this door, and not very long ago. Which was odd, as the house had been deserted for more than a hundred years. Katie pressed one eye to the clear section of glass and peeked inside.

The large, high-ceilinged entrance hall was dark and lifeless. Empty. As her eye adjusted to the half-light, Katie saw a staircase emerge from the gloom. It swept up and to the right, with wooden banisters supported by white spindle posts. Then, on the far side of the staircase, she pale, ghostlike figures, more and more of them, slowly took shape.

Her heart fluttered in her chest, and Katie was about to take off when she suddenly realized what the shapes must be. Sometimes they showed closed-up houses like this on TV, with white sheets draped over pieces of furniture to protect them from dust. Any old house might have them.

Even so, what odd-looking furniture it must be! There were no long or low items that might be sofas or tables or even chairs. It looked more like a group of shrouded people — men, women, children, even a small one about the size of a puppy. Weird.

Her breath caught in her throat. Did one of the sheets just move? Couldn't have. There it went again! Closest to the door, tall and ghostly white, a sheet shape crept steadily toward her.

For the first time in her life Katie caught up to Sheila. She almost tripped over her friend's heels as the two girls raced along the pathway. Her heart hammered against her ribs so hard she couldn't breathe. She reached the open gate, ran through it and skidded to a stop. As she stood there trying to catch her breath, Katie knew running had been a big mistake. Slowly she turned to look back at the house.

Nothing. Quiet and still, it stared vacantly back at her.

A rush of embarrassment washed over Katie as she realized what she had done. Furniture, even furniture with sheets draped over it, does not move on its own. What she saw must have been a trick of the sunlight sparkling through glass, perhaps the swaying shadow of a nearby tree branch. But now, because of her, Sheila and Rusty would refuse to come down here ever again. She glanced at the two of them. They stared back, frozen, their eyes wide and mouths gaping.

"What happened?" Rusty whispered.

"Nothing," Katie shrugged, and glanced down at her feet. "Oh, I hate these stupid shoelaces!" She bent to do them up. They seemed to constantly come undone. Picking up her knapsack, she avoided Rusty's eyes. "Anyone ready for lunch?"

"Sure," said Rusty. "I'm starved! Let's go down to the beach. I haven't eaten for hours!"

Sheila said nothing but led the way to the top of the bank, pushing her bike. Rusty followed close behind. Both of them were walking rapidly, as if they were being chased.

Katie narrowed her eyes. Something was wrong. Those two should demand to go somewhere else — anywhere else — to eat lunch, they had been so scared of coming here in the first place. Instead, they laid down their bikes and disappeared over the bank. Why were they in such a big hurry to get to the beach? Did they know something she didn't know?

Katie pushed her bike to the top of the bank and

peered over. Sheila had taken off her jacket and was crouched now on a rocky outcrop. She leaned forward and dipped her arms, right up to the elbows, in salt water. At the bottom of the bank, Rusty picked himself up, attempted to brush fresh dirt off the seat of his jeans, gave up and hurried over to join Sheila.

"Should we do our faces too?" she asked him.

"Yes — just to be on the safe side," Rusty advised her.

Puzzled, Katie scrambled down the bank. The others were so busy leaning over and splashing water on their faces, they did not see her coming. When she was close behind them, she demanded, "What's going on around here?"

Rusty jumped, fell back, and started sliding down the seaweed-slick rock. He was in water up to his knees when, swift as a pouncing cat, Sheila grabbed his arm. She helped him up.

Rusty turned and scowled at Katie. "What are you trying to do, drown me? The mud puddle was too shallow? So now you're trying to dump me in the sea. I know you don't like having me tag along, but that's no reason to try and do me in!"

"Don't be dumb, Rusty. You've been reading too many murder mysteries lately, you think everyone's out to get you. Besides, you don't need any help falling in the water — you do it all by yourself." She paused. "But I can't figure out why you two are so crazy about washing all of a sudden."

Rusty blurted, "It's the legend …"

"Just getting cleaned up for lunch," Sheila interrupted him. "You should too."

"Why? You never did before!" Katie zeroed in on Rusty's face. He knew something, and she was determined to find out what it was.

He stared back at her, at a loss for a good answer. Wet, muddy, and with shiny green chunks of sea lettuce decorating his jeans and running shoes, he tried very hard to look serious. He must have realized it wouldn't work because he quickly changed the subject. "I'm starved," he said, and started for the beach.

Katie watched him go. The beach faced a tiny, protected inlet, not much bigger than a large swimming pool. On the opposite shore was a steep hillside covered in tall firs and cedars that completely hid the inlet from the road above. Behind the beach was a rocky finger of high ground, a small peninsula that curved back gently toward the hillside, allowing only a narrow opening from the inlet to the sea. It was scarcely wide enough for a boat to squeeze through, especially now, with the tide so low. The house stood in the middle of the peninsula, behind them, and was almost completely hidden from the road.

A fat, wet cormorant flapped across the smooth water and finally managed to take off. Katie looked from the bird to a tiny, weather-beaten wharf that floated crookedly on the surface, jutting out into the water. "Let's go see if there are any fish under there," she suggested.

"I'm too hungry," Rusty said, stopping to look back. "Anyway, it doesn't look very safe to me. I bet it's falling apart. You should stay off it."

If they had been undecided, Rusty's unwelcome advice was enough to help them make up their minds. Katie and Sheila headed for the wharf.

Close up, it looked surprisingly sturdy. Shiny new nails held the boards to the logs on each side. All the wood seemed strong and solid in spite of its weathered, gray appearance. The girls knelt beside one of the pilings that held the wharf in place and leaned forward to peer down through the square hole into clear, green water.

Something was wrong.

Katie's head jerked up. Sheila's huge eyes stared back at Katie, her face so white that the brown freckles stood out even more clearly than usual.

Both girls leaned over for a second look. Above high-tide level the piling was gray and weathered, but the tar that protected it underwater was as smooth and black as the day it had been painted on. Not a barnacle, not a sea anemone, not a trace of weed grew on it.

"This wharf is brand new," Sheila whispered. "Someone's been here!"

... two ...

The Legend

Rusty had settled in the sun on a sandy patch of beach and leaned happily against a big log, munching on a piece of leftover pizza. He licked his greasy lips.

Katie leaned closer to Sheila. "Don't tell Rusty about the wharf," she warned. "He'll never want to come here again."

Sheila nodded.

The beach was hot, protected from a cool wind that blew off the strait. Katie sat on a patch of sand in front of the log and took off her jacket, running shoes, and socks. She dug her toes into warm, powdery sand.

"So," she said, biting into a peanut butter and banana sandwich. "What's this about a legend?"

"You'll never believe it!" Rusty began, and then made a gulping sound in his throat. His eyes flicked guiltily over to Sheila.

Katie pressed her lips together, annoyed that Sheila

didn't want Rusty to talk to her. Sheila was supposed to be her friend, not Rusty's. "I'm going to find out sooner or later," she pointed out, "so you might as well tell me now."

Sheila picked up a rock and tossed it into the water.

Rusty glanced back at Katie, thought for a moment, and made up his mind. He took a deep breath. "Okay. Remember when you went to the dentist yesterday?"

Katie nodded.

"Well, that's when I told Sheila about it."

"Sheila came over when I was at the dentist?"

"Yeah, well, she forgot you were busy. Anyhow, I told her about this ship that smashed on the rocks in a storm a long time ago and all the crew drowned and they buried them up there." He glanced over Katie's shoulder and shuddered. Perhaps to reassure himself, he shoved a whole chocolate brownie into his mouth.

"Who did?"

Rusty rolled his eyes. He couldn't speak, his mouth was so full. Finally he swallowed. "Some Native people. See, I asked my dad about the haunted house and all when you kept bugging us to come here." He stopped to lick chocolate from his fingers. "So anyway, he looked it up in the archives."

"A fun place to work," Katie remarked.

"He likes it," Rusty said happily, "and I'm going to be an archivist when I grow up too. Anyway, my dad said the Natives used to tell a story about a schooner that came to these waters when hardly any white people lived here.

They described exactly what it looked like: three masts, triangular sails rigged fore and aft — they even claimed it had a flag with a skull and crossbones on it."

"So they were pirates!" Katie held up her cup and tipped her head back to let the last drop of lemonade drip onto her tongue.

"Maybe. It sure sounds like it. Anyway, they were really mean, and the Natives hated them. They used to come into Native villages and take whatever they wanted. The Natives had a few guns by then, but nothing like the big guns and cannons on the schooner.

"So anyway, one night the pirate ship got caught in a big storm and smashed against a rock on the other side." He jerked his head backward, indicating the seaward side of the peninsula.

"And they all drowned," added Katie, picturing a treasure chest half buried in sand with shiny little kelp perch swimming around it.

Rusty shook his head. "No one knows whether they all drowned or the Natives finished them off. Maybe some of them even escaped into the woods. But the Natives buried most of them up there. The bones might be right underneath the house. No one knows for sure."

Katie waited, hardly able to sit still, while Rusty nibbled thoughtfully on another brownie. *That's it?* she finally asked. "Not much of a legend, if you ask me."

"Legend?" Rusty popped the brownie into his mouth and avoided her eyes. He stole a quick glance at Sheila, who stood up and strolled to the water's edge, carrying a half-eaten bagel with her. She bent to pick up a flat stone, hauled off and skipped it expertly across the smooth blue surface of the inlet.

Rusty leaned closer to Katie and whispered, "Okay, here's what happened. After the Natives buried all the dead pirates, they were covered in dirt and blood and junk like that. So they decided to go down to the beach and clean up. But two of the village elders — one was the chief — waited up top.

"When the others climbed back up, the elders were nowhere in sight. The wind was howling and the waves were crashing against the rocks, they searched for hours and couldn't find them. Finally they decided to go back to the village and see if the men had gone on ahead. But no one at the village had seen them. In fact … no one ever saw them again!"

"Maybe some of the pirates killed them," Katie suggested.

"Or maybe some of the pirates' ghosts!" Rusty said breathlessly, leaning even closer.

Katie narrowed her eyes at him. He pulled away.

"So, who built the house here?" she demanded.

"See, more than a hundred years ago this guy, Sir Charles Matthews, came out from England to build a mansion for his bride — he wanted to impress her, I guess. It impressed her, all right!" He stopped and glanced toward Sheila.

She had wandered down the beach and was tossing stones over the inlet. Katie tried not to look envious, even though she could never throw a stone anywhere near that far if she tried all day.

"What happened?" She wished he would just get on with the story and stop looking at Sheila.

"Okay." Rusty drew a deep breath. "First of all, they had big problems building the house. One day the floor gave way and some men fell through. Another time a beam crashed down and killed a workman. Then the construction foreman disappeared."

"Weird." Katie wondered what any of this had to do with today.

"Finally, somebody remembered the old story. See, the Natives believed evil spirits had carried away the elders. They thought this whole peninsula was under the control of the pirates' ghosts. So if any Native people needed to come near here, they would always wash very carefully in the salt water before they left."

"Brrr," said Katie, thinking of the cold salt water.

"Yeah, but most of the coastal Natives believed in a ritual cleansing to get close to the good spirits. So, I guess they figured that the best way to ward off evil spirits was to wash like crazy and ask for protection. Besides, all the Natives who survived that first night had washed in the sea."

"So," said Katie, "I guess it's kind of like getting baptized."

Rusty frowned and shook his head before continuing. "Anyway, one of the workmen decided to wash his hands and face in the sea every night before he went home. All the other men laughed at him. Every night while he was washing, they stood on the bank, teasing him and calling him dumb names."

Katie nodded. "Just like boys do."

Rusty frowned again. "Then one night when they were standing there, a huge Douglas fir suddenly started to topple over and came crashing toward them. The man on the beach saw it and yelled just in time for the others to scramble out of the way. It thundered to the ground and shook the earth as they ran. But they didn't stop. They ran straight into the water and splashed it all over themselves as if they were on fire. After that they practically tripped over each other to get down to the beach and wash every night. I bet they were the cleanest people in town! And they never had any more problems with the construction."

Katie laughed. "So that's why you two were so busy washing!"

Rusty scowled at her. "It never hurts to be clean! You should try it sometime."

Katie ignored that. "Did the people ever move into the house?"

"Yes, but not for long. By the time they had been here a few months, all the servants except one loyal butler had run off. Some people say he sneaked down to the beach every night to wash and so he knew he was safe.

"The cook moved into a little house in town and told stories about eerie sounds coming from underneath the kitchen at this place. The gardener insisted he saw two old Native men and two pirates on a dark, stormy night fighting just up there." He pointed up the bank above their heads. Katie followed his gaze to a huge fallen tree. Its gnarled and tangled roots had been washed clean by heavy rains and bleached white by years of sun.

"Some imagination!" Katie snickered.

Rusty ignored her and continued his story. "One cold, windy night Sir Charles disappeared. The next day someone found his wife on the beach in her long night-gown. She was soaking wet and blue with cold. She didn't even know where she was. They put her in the hospital, and she got really sick with pneumonia. She raved on and on about stolen treasure and voices coming from beneath the ground.

"Well, Dr. Helmcken cured her pneumonia, but that didn't stop her from raving on like a crazy lady. The doctor's father-in-law was James Douglas — you know, governor of Vancouver Island? Anyway, the two of them got together and decided to put her on a ship and send her back to her family in England."

Rusty paused. He reached for another brownie. Katie snatched them away.

"And?" she demanded.

"Okay. This is the weird part. The night before her ship was to sail, she vanished! They never found a trace of her. They finally decided she was so upset about losing her husband that she threw herself off a cliff into the sea."

"Wow!" said Katie. "And the house has been empty ever since?"

Rusty nodded. "Just about. A couple of times a nephew or some other relative who inherited the house from the lady came out here for a while. One of them even started to paint it — that's the undercoat on it now. But every one of them took off before very long. Scared, I guess. English people believe in ghosts, you know."

Katie looked out over the inlet, thinking about what Rusty had told her. "I bet that's why you decided to come down here with me today," she said. "Because you found out all that history about the place."

Rusty shrugged. "It's interesting," he said. "All those people who vanished …"

As Rusty spoke, a gust of wind rippled across the inlet. Katie felt its icy touch as though cold, ethereal fingers had brushed softly against her skin. A chill tingled down her spine.

The wind had shifted. It blew full force now through the narrow opening of the inlet, whipping up waves and splashing them against the shore. A dark cloud blotted out the sun. Sheila came striding toward them. "Let's go to my house," she said. "It's going to rain."

Katie carefully inspected her hands. Definitely quite sticky. And she was sure she must have chocolate on her face like Rusty did.

"You two go ahead," she said as she hurried toward the water. "I'll just be a minute."

Katie stepped onto a big rock and crouched to dip her hands in the water, rubbing them vigorously. She was splashing seawater on her face when she noticed the silence. Glancing over her shoulder, she saw the other two standing with their hands on their hips, watching her, grinning.

"What?" She looked at her hands, bright red from the cold water, and stepped back to the beach. "They were sticky!" But the others kept on grinning. "If you want to ride home with peanut butter on your hands and chocolate all over your faces, that's up to you." She shoved her feet into her shoes, zipped up her jacket and wriggled into her knapsack. "But I think you just look dumb!"

She marched away from them just as the rain began to fall.

... three ...

The Fort

Raindrops bounced off the slick pavement as the three pedaled toward Sheila's house. When the road curved up and over a hill, Sheila effortlessly pulled into the lead.

Katie strained for breath, trying to catch up to Sheila, struggling to widen the distance between herself and Rusty. A few minutes later she turned onto Sheila's street, just a block away from the sea. The peaceful, tree-lined avenue was deserted. Behind the spreading branches of tall chestnut trees, huge, old houses were set well back from the road behind low stone walls or neatly clipped hedges. Wedged between two of these giants, Sheila's house, a square, box-like house with a tiny front lawn and a cement sidewalk leading to the front door, seemed even smaller than it really was. Katie turned onto the narrower sidewalk that ran beside the house to Sheila's backyard.

Her friend waited under the shelter of the overhang as Katie rode up and jumped off her bike. Out of breath and trying desperately to hide it, she made a show of leaning her bike behind Sheila's against the pale yellow stucco while she took in great gulps of air. When Rusty arrived, the three of them hurried to the back porch, where they kicked off their soggy shoes and stepped into the friendly little kitchen.

"Hi, girls!" a voice called.

"Hi, Mom! Rusty's here too. What's to eat?" Sheila padded into the living room with the other two trailing behind.

"Rusty?" Seated on the couch with her feet up, Ms. Walton looked up from pouring herself some tea. Her puzzled look changed to a smile. "Oh, Russell! I haven't seen you since last summer! How are you doing?"

"Russ," he corrected. "I'm Okay."

"How's your dad, Russ? Still slaving away down there at the archives?"

"Yup."

"Good. Well, help yourselves to some chocolate chip cookies." She nodded toward the cookie tin on the table and gave a tired sigh. "I just got home from work. What have you three been up to?"

Her amber eyes wandered over the motley group. Elaine Walton had an attractive, friendly face with a fine sprinkling of pale freckles; her very short auburn hair was brushed back from her face. She was a tall, athletic woman who looked very impressive in her police uniform. Her eyes stopped at Rusty, at his dirt-streaked face, the mud on his clothes, the little bits of seaweed, and she opened her mouth as if to ask a question. Instead, she snapped it shut again and pressed her lips together. Fine wrinkles appeared at the corners of her eyes.

"Just went for a bike ride." Sheila ran her fingers through her hair, so sleek and soft that even wearing a bike helmet didn't mess it up.

Katie tried to press down her unruly curls.

"We went to the haunted house," Rusty added.

Furrows appeared between Elaine Walton's eyebrows. "You mean that old place down on the point?"

Rusty nodded.

"Why did you go there?"

He shrugged. "It was Katie's idea."

Ms. Walton turned to Katie; her eyebrows formed a question.

Katie studied her socks. She felt like kicking her cousin in the shins, and would have, too, if she'd been wearing shoes. "I just wanted to have a look."

"And did you see anything interesting?"

Katie pictured the white shape moving toward her. "No, not really."

"You know, it's strange, but every once in a while we get reports from people who insist they've heard odd noises or even seen ghosts down there. I can't figure out why. It's not during a full moon or anything, it just happens all of a sudden. For two or three nights we'll get maybe a dozen phone calls. Then everything will be quiet again."

"Have you had any calls lately?" Katie asked, suddenly interested.

Sheila's mom nodded. "I'll say. More than usual. For the past week we've been getting several calls a night. People claim they hear noises — like hammering — and see lights and white shapes moving around in the dark."

Rusty shuddered. "I told you we shouldn't go down there."

"Do you go and investigate when you get calls?" Katie asked.

"I never have. But a couple of officers often take a drive by when they're in the neighborhood, even though the chief told us not to bother. They've never found a thing — we chalk it up to overactive imaginations."

"Did they go this time?"

"Spike Davis and Archie McFee drove down last night. Sheila knows them — they sometimes stop by for coffee when I'm off duty. According to them, there's no sign of life down there — and not a single ghost either! It's a good thing too, because I really don't know how they would handcuff one." She chose a cookie and sat back, chuckling to herself. The kids stared at her blankly.

"I hope they washed their hands and faces," Rusty said into the silence.

Ms. Walton bit into her cookie. She chewed thoughtfully, studying Rusty as if she wasn't quite sure she had heard correctly. "People have been calling it the haunted house for a hundred years or more," she said. "And they've been imagining sights and sounds there for just as long. Chief Carlson doesn't want us wasting police time on crank calls like that."

· · · · · ·

By the time the three sat down to cookies and hot chocolate in the kitchen, the rain had stopped. Before they finished eating, the sun was shining again. They decided to go and check out their fort. None of them had been there since last summer.

"Can't you keep quiet about that stupid legend?" Katie said to Rusty the minute they stepped outside.

"Why should I? I don't want anyone to disappear."

"What do you think people will do when you tell them to wash in the sea so pirates' ghosts won't get them?"

Rusty shrugged and climbed onto his bike. "I don't know."

"They'll laugh, that's what. They'll think you're just a dumb kid."

· · · · · ·

The high rock wall twisted alongside a road so narrow, so winding, and so steep that longer cars had difficulty making the turns as they drove up it. Traffic was one way — up only. Apparently it was too dangerous to drive down, although Katie's mother insisted she used to ride down it on her bike when she was a kid. Near the bottom, the road widened and straightened out. At that point the rock wall ended, and a chain-link fence continued down the hill to Richardson Street. The three locked their bikes to a tree on the boulevard opposite the fence.

They ran up the winding road and darted around the first curve, out of sight of nearby houses. Then they pulled themselves onto the rock wall with the help of pointed rocks embedded upright along each side of the wide top, giving it the look of a medieval castle. Once on the top, they turned and climbed down the other side. They worked their way through tall grass, under the wide-spreading branches of Garry oak and over rock outcroppings, until they finally stopped in front of a tiny, rather crooked structure built of scrap two-by-fours and odd pieces of plywood Katie had borrowed from her father when he was not looking. When they had run out of boards, they had substituted branches and pieces of bark. Most of the leafy branches that once acted as camouflage had blown away over the winter, and the fort was now clearly visible, nestled snugly between two oak trees. The sturdy trunks helped hold it up while the thick, dark green leaves of smaller oaks provided a little privacy.

The canvas door still hung in place but was dirty now and green with moss that grew thick on the bottom of it. Katie pushed the door back and they all trooped inside. Their old, rusty lawn chairs were still there, a little older and rustier now. They were arranged around a tree stump that served as a table.

"There was something funny about that house," Rusty said as soon as they sat down.

"What?" Katie asked.

"See, when we got to the fort, it reminded me. There

was this big pile of branches that just didn't look natural — like they weren't really growing there at all. I bet something was hidden under them."

"Maybe the ghosts built themselves a fort," Katie suggested, grinning.

He stuck out his tongue. "Very funny!"

Katie pulled her notebook from her knapsack and started to write. "Did you notice those tire tracks at the top of the road?" she asked. "They were quite fresh, but it looked like someone tried to wipe them away."

Not to be outdone, Sheila turned to Rusty. "You know that wharf?"

Katie's head jerked up.

Rusty nodded.

"Well, it's really strong, as if someone just built it, but they want it to look old. And there aren't any weeds or barnacles underneath."

Katie scowled at the back of her friend's head. "You forgot to mention the scrapes in the wood on the wharf."

Sheila turned to her, a blank look on her face.

"Oh, didn't you see them? There were marks just like them on the front porch of the house. I think we should go back tomorrow and investigate," Katie said.

She glanced up at the sign hanging crookedly over the canvas door. Painted by Rusty, it showed a cat peeping over a clump of grass, and underneath, the fancy lettering read: Investigations Unlimited. "I mean, we always wanted a real mystery to solve."

"I'll be there," said Rusty. "Mom isn't working

tomorrow, but I'll ride my bike over. Someone has to keep the two of you out of trouble."

"Oh, sure, Rusty," said Katie, "and who's the one who landed in a mud puddle and slipped into the water today? Not to mention falling down the bank."

Rusty squirmed. "Don't call me Rusty."

"Why not? It goes so well with Gates. Russ Gates just doesn't work for me."

"Now, children, let's not argue," said Sheila in a very grown-up voice, "or we won't be able to go to the house tomorrow."

Katie glared at her, then smiled happily. "So it's decided. We all go to the house."

Now, if she could just figure out how to get them *inside* the house.

... four ...

The Chief

A robin chirped outside; puddles of sunlight dappled the floor beneath her curtains; the rich scent of warm earth wafted through the open window. Katie lay in bed, wanting to sleep but unable to stop her mind from turning round and round in circles, churning out the same questions over and over again. Why would anyone want to make a new wharf look old? What could have made the strange scrapes and smudges? Had she only imagined that the white shape was creeping toward her? What were those white figures, anyway? What were the noises people heard? And, most importantly, what would happen if she went inside the house?

A strange kind of fear gripped her, and she knew she could not go in alone. Of course, Rusty would never go with her. Even if he did, he would probably fall through a floor or tumble down the stairs, and they would need to call 911 to get him out again. That left only Sheila.

Katie got up, dressed and plodded upstairs to the kitchen, feeling very important, as if she were already a private investigator, soon to be known and admired throughout the entire world.

"Did you remember to tidy your room?" her mother asked as Katie stepped into the kitchen.

Katie rolled her eyes. If her mother only knew the truth, she would not bother her with such trivial matters. "I thought it was tidy already."

Her mom's eyebrows shot up and her dark brown eyes turned thoughtful. "That's odd, because last night it looked as if you had been burglarized."

"Oh, that. Well, I think it was Michael. He comes down and takes things …"

"Tidy it up before you go out," her mom said firmly, and handed Katie a big jar of homemade granola.

Katie sat down and poured some into a bowl. Halfway through her breakfast, she glanced at the clock and realized it was almost time to meet the others. Taking the bowl with her, she darted downstairs, tossed dirty socks and underwear into her closet, shoved a half-eaten bag of corn chips under the bed, pulled her comforter over the rumpled sheets and picked up two dirty glasses. Where could they go? In her empty sock drawer, of course. Good. Done. She grabbed her knapsack and ran upstairs, still shoveling granola into her mouth. She packed some lunch, told her mom she was off to Sheila's and ran out the door.

• • • • • •

They stopped near the top of Rotten Road. Katie leapt off her bike and crouched to examine the dirt road. "There are new tracks!" she announced. "They must have been made after the rain stopped last night."

She moved farther down the hill, taking small steps, studying the road. "Someone tried to smooth them over, but that's hard to do in mud. Look at the tread marks down here."

There, in the soft mud, were clear imprints of wide tires, made by a heavy vehicle. But close to the main road the marks had been smoothed over with some sort of flat object. Passersby would never know that any vehicle had gone down there recently.

"Let's go down!" said Rusty. "I'll show you where the piled-up bushes are." He jumped on his bike and started down the narrow dirt road.

Sheila waited while Katie walked back to her bike and started to pick it up. She put it down again. "I hate these shoelaces!" she said, and bent to retie them. By the time she and Sheila reached the bottom of the hill, Rusty was leaning awkwardly against his bike, gazing wide-eyed at a tangle of thistles and tall grass to the left of the house. "They were here yesterday," he insisted. "I saw them!"

He dropped his bike, pushed past the gate and hurried to the spot. Trudging back and forth, he thrust aside tall weeds and studied the ground. Suddenly he stopped and bent over. "Look at this!"

The others ran to see. On the dark soil, almost hidden by weeds, was a black, sticky stain. Rusty touched it, then sniffed his fingers. "Oil," he said. "Something has been parked here and covered over. I know it! A car or truck, and they hid it so no one would know and then —"

"They uncovered it and went away," Katie interrupted. "Which proves," she counted on her fingers, "one, they aren't ghosts, and two, they aren't here now. So, let's go look inside."

They headed for the house together. At the foot of the stairs, Rusty came to an abrupt halt. Sheila and Katie continued swiftly up to the verandah, where they each found an eye-sized pane of clear glass to peek through.

At first they saw nothing, but as their eyes adjusted from the brightness outside to the gloom inside the house, Katie slowly realized that something had changed. The entrance hall and wide, sweeping staircase were the same, but there was no sign of the white, shrouded figures that had stood in that same hall only a day earlier.

A sudden movement caught her eye. The flicker of a shadow, then the shape of a man appeared in a doorway beyond the stairs. He was tall and stood very straight. His shoulders were broad and muscular. He wore blue jeans and a white shirt with the sleeves rolled up. His steel gray hair was styled so perfectly that he could have been a movie star, and his deep-set black eyes darted about the room. A shaft of sunlight from some unseen window caught the bright glitter of a gold chain at his neck. The man looked directly toward the front door.

Katie froze. Deep frown lines appeared on the man's forehead. From each side of his nose a heavy crease curved down to the corner of his mouth. He started walking toward the door. Katie's feet were cement blocks, and her heart pounded so hard she was positive it would burst.

The man swung sharply to his right and disappeared. Sheila gave a funny squeak that seemed to come from her throat, turned and ran down the stairs, with Katie right behind her. They flew past a surprised Rusty and straight for the beach. Sheila was at the bottom of the bank and Katie partway down when Rusty tumbled past her. He jumped to his feet, and all three ran splashing into the water.

"What happened?" Rusty demanded.

Knee deep in cold water, Katie suddenly stopped splashing it over her face and arms. She glanced around. Sheila and Rusty were washing as though their lives depended on it. Katie pushed back her curls with her wet hands. She did not believe in ghosts — even so, if she ever tried to imagine what a Native chief might look like, that craggy-faced man, in spite of his modern clothing and hairdo, would be it. She waded out of the water and sat on a rock. "That's so stupid!" she said.

"You were in here too," Rusty reminded her. "What happened?"

"Nothing — we just got spooked, I guess."

But he would not be put off. "You saw something. I want to know what."

"There was someone up there," Sheila told him. "In the house."

"Someone? Like who? You looked like you saw a ghost."

"It wasn't a ghost, just a man," Katie explained.

"A man — in the house? What did he look like?"

She shrugged. "I don't know, kind of old and wrinkled. Probably just someone looking for a place to sleep."

"So — he looked like a bum?"

Katie hesitated, thinking of the gold necklace. "I guess so," she said. "Yeah, kind of like a rich bum."

"Well, I say we get out of here. And fast."

For once Katie agreed with her cousin. "Okay. Let's go to Sheila's."

• • • • • •

They piled their lunches on Sheila's kitchen table. Katie perched on the edge of a chair and bent over her notebook. "Gray hair," she wrote, "gold necklace, dark, scary eyes." Sheila stood at the counter making three chocolate milks. Except for his thoughtful munching of potato chips, Rusty was strangely quiet. Then, quite suddenly, he said, "Tell me what he looks like and I'll draw a picture."

Sheila turned from the counter. "A composite drawing?"

"Yeah, I guess so. Like the police do."

"Good idea," Sheila told him. "Maybe we can find out who he is."

"Or was," Rusty added, stuffing more potato chips

into his mouth. He wiped his hand on his shorts and reached into his knapsack. He pulled out a flashlight, a dirty sock, and something unrecognizable wrapped in plastic before he found his sketchbook and a pencil. He turned to a clean page. "Shape of face."

"Round," said Katie.

"Square," said Sheila at exactly the same time.

Rusty glanced from one to the other, his eyebrows pulled together.

"Well, sort of square with round corners," Katie told him.

Sheila nodded. She poured milk into the glasses while Rusty sketched. "Like this?" he asked, holding up the sketchbook.

Sheila nodded. Katie shrugged.

"Eyes?"

"Squinty," said Katie.

"Round," said Sheila.

"They were really dark," Katie said, and Sheila agreed.

They stood behind Rusty and managed to agree on the eyes — round in the middle and squinty at the edges. The heavy, black eyebrows that almost met over his nose, the steel gray hair and the deep furrow between his eyes were no problem, but when it came to describing his nose, they could only agree that it was big. Sheila thought it was long and flat; Katie insisted it stuck out and had a bump in the middle.

Rusty grumbled under his breath as he erased his tenth nose. "Let's try the mouth," he suggested.

"I wonder where I've seen him before," Sheila murmured as she walked over to add chocolate to the milk.

"What?" Katie demanded.

A silvery tinkle of spoon against glass was the only sound in the room. Sheila picked up two frosty glasses foaming with chocolate milk, turned and met two pairs of eyes staring at her. "He just looks familiar, that's all."

"Why didn't you tell us before?" Katie asked.

"I don't know," Sheila shrugged as she placed the glasses on the table.

"If you ask me —" Rusty sat back and squinted at his sketch "— I think he looks like an old Native chief. I bet you saw his picture in a history book at school. You know, from before he disappeared?"

"He wasn't a ghost. Sheila studied the sketch. "He was real."

"You never know for sure till you touch them," Rusty informed her confidently.

"Sure, Rusty," said Katie.

"Russ," he corrected.

Katie ran her fingers through her curls, trying to remember exactly what the man's mouth looked like. "His lips were kind of thin and mean looking, like he was mad at somebody. Right?" She turned hopefully to Sheila.

"Kind of. Make them turn down in the corners." Sheila stirred chocolate into her own glass and picked it up. The doorbell rang. She carried the glass with her to answer it.

Katie jumped up when she heard the crash, the splintering of glass. She glanced at Rusty, but his head was bent over his work and he didn't appear to notice.

Katie couldn't see the front door, but she heard it slam shut so hard that the house shuddered around her. She broke into a run.

Sheila's back was pressed up against the door, her eyes wild with fear. A chocolate brown pool spread out near her feet. It was filled with little islands of broken glass.

"What's going on?" Katie demanded.

Sheila's answer was barely audible. "It's him! Rusty was right!"

"Who? About what?"

"He must have followed us! I opened the door, he said," her voice went suddenly deep, " 'Hi, I'm the Chief' — see if he's still there!"

Katie walked toward the large living room window to her right. It overlooked the stairs and front yard.

"Don't let him see you!" Sheila hissed.

Obligingly, Katie dropped to her knees, crawled to the window and pulled herself up to peek over the sill. A tall, gray-haired man wearing jeans and a white shirt was walking down the sidewalk away from the house, pushing a shiny mountain bike. He glanced back at the front door, shaking his head. Katie ducked.

"You're right! It's him! But how did he find us?"

"Who knows? What's he doing?"

"I think he's leaving."

They heard a car approaching. It slowed to a stop.

"What now?" Sheila hadn't moved from the door.

"Must be another ghost," said Katie. "I didn't know they drove cars."

"Not funny."

The engine stopped. A car door slammed. Voices floated back toward the house. A minute later footsteps started up the stairs. Katie pulled herself up to peek out. "It's your mom! He's coming in with her! And he has his hand on her arm."

Sheila whirled around. "I've got to save her!" She waited, listening, until the footsteps reached the front porch. Then she flung the door open. "Mom, quick, get inside!"

"What's the hurry?" her mom asked, glancing up at the sky as if she expected something to come crashing down around her ears. "And why did you slam the door in Chief Carlson's face?" she asked crossly. "He just happened to be riding by and stopped in to say hello."

"Chief Carlson?" Sheila whispered.

"Yes, the chief of police — my boss."

... five ...

Too Many Questions

Ms. Walton edged around the sticky mess on the floor. Her eyes narrowed; she looked closely at Sheila as if to assure herself this really was her daughter.

"Hi, Katie," she sighed as Katie popped up from her vantage point by the window. "Perhaps you girls could put on some coffee after you clean up this mess."

Sheila got a bucket of water and some rags and the two girls set to work while Sheila's mother and Chief Carlson settled on chairs in the living room. They were so quiet Katie knew they were watching every move she and Sheila made. The girls picked out all the tiny shards of broken glass and then started to wipe up the sticky liquid. In no time the rags were saturated with chocolate milk.

"I'll rinse them and get some clean water," Katie offered.

Moments later, as she stepped from the bathroom

with a bucket of fresh water in one hand and two damp rags in the other, Rusty passed in front of her. She stopped and put down the pail. "Stop!" she whispered, but Rusty didn't hear.

"Check out this nose," he said to Sheila, raising his sketchbook. "I made it long, with a bump in the middle, and I gave him wide, flat nostrils."

The low hum of conversation in the living room died.

Sheila, on her knees near the door, glanced up. Her eyes widened, her mouth opened, but no sound came out. She shook her head and raised a warning hand.

One more step, and Rusty would be in full view of the chief of police and Sheila's mother. So would his composite drawing!

Katie had to stop him. "CATCH!" she yelled, and threw the damp rags one after the other at Rusty's sketchbook. The first one hit it squarely in the middle, knocking it from his hands. He whirled around just in time to catch the second rag across his face. He staggered back, slipped on the spilt milk, and his feet went out from under him. He landed sprawled flat on his back, looking up at Sheila.

"Hey!" Rusty peeled the wet rag off his face. "What'd you do that for?"

"Good question," said Elaine Walton.

Rusty turned slowly at the sound of her voice. He looked first at Sheila's mom, then at her companion. Finally, he glanced down at his soggy drawing, beside him on the floor. It bore a remarkable likeness to the chief of police. "Whoa!" he said, and scrambled to his feet. "Hey, Ms. W.!" he grinned idiotically. "Well, I'm outta here," he said as he fled past Katie to the kitchen, carrying his sketchbook.

Katie followed him.

"I'm gone," he said, stuffing his sketchbook and assorted junk into his knapsack and opening the back door.

"Wait, Rusty. It's not what you think — he's the chief of police, not a Native chief."

"I don't care if he's the chief *librarian*. I'm going home." He slammed the door behind him.

"I think you'd better go too, Katie," said a quiet voice.

Katie swung around to see Ms. Walton standing in the doorway, hands on her hips. She did not look happy.

"Chief Carlson decided to leave," she said. "And I need to talk to Sheila alone."

"But it's my fault …"

Ms. Walton shook her head.

Katie tried again. "The mess …"

"Sheila will clean it up. Off you go now, Katie." Ms. Walton picked up Katie's knapsack, handed it to her and ushered her toward the door.

"You can call Sheila tomorrow," Katie heard as the door closed behind her.

• • • • • •

Later that afternoon, Katie settled back on a lounge chair in her backyard. A mystery novel was propped against her bent knees, but she could not concentrate on it. Questions kept bouncing back and forth in her head. Why was the chief of police snooping around the old house? Maybe he wanted to investigate the reports. But why? He'd told the other officers not to waste their time down there.

Katie had no idea what a police chief did all day, but she imagined he was a lot like her school principal. He probably sat behind a desk, holding a pen in one hand and staring sadly at stacks of papers. Every once in a while the phone would ring and he would talk for a while. Then he would move a few papers around and stare at them some more. For this he would get paid more money than anyone else who worked there. Which meant his time was more valuable. So why would he waste his time at the house if the ordinary officers were supposed to stay away? And why had he "just happened" to come by Sheila's house? Was it a coincidence? Did he follow them?

Cold water splashed over her stomach. She sat up. "You little brat!"

From high above, Michael's face grinned down at her. His arms and legs were wrapped around a thin branch of a cedar tree. In his hand was a squirt gun, pointed at her. Michael's short curly hair glowed golden in a ray of sunshine that shone through a break in the foliage.

Her brother was small for his seven years and thin, with long, bony legs, not at all sturdy like his older sister. "I thought you looked hot," he said, "so I cooled you off. When are you going skating with me?"

Would he ever stop bugging her about that? Once,

to please their mother, she had taken him in-line skating. Now he wanted her to go all the time. "I told you, never! And don't you dare squirt me again or I'll get you."

"Ha!" he said. "I can climb so high you'll never catch me!"

He pulled himself up to stand on the branch, then shinnied easily up the tree trunk to a higher, thinner perch. There he settled and started singing "Row, Row, Row Your Boat" over and over in his squeaky, annoying voice.

"Go away," said Katie. "How am I supposed to think?"

"What're you thinking about?"

"Nothing!"

"Oh," he said, "then that's easy. I'll just keep on singing till you're done." He sang a little more, then stopped abruptly. "Katie, if you're not thinking about anything, how will you know when you're done?"

· · · · · ·

In the evening, Katie sprawled on the couch in the family room, trying to read but wishing she could call Sheila. She didn't dare. Sheila's mother was mad at her for the way she had treated Rusty. Katie felt bad about that.

Her dad came in and flicked on the TV. She peeked over her book. The news was on and a woman journalist was introducing someone. The camera swung to him. Katie dropped her book. The camera returned to the journalist.

"The recent rash of robberies involving valuable art objects and museum pieces has the police stumped. Tell me, Chief Carlson, are you any closer to a solution?"

The camera focused on the craggy face of the chief of police. "My detectives are working round the clock on this case. There are several leads they are following at the moment."

The camera swung to a picture of the missing sculptures. To Katie, they were strange-looking objects of twisted wire and metal. She studied them, trying to figure out why anyone would consider them valuable. She yawned, and the sculptures blurred. Now she saw them covered with sheets, standing like statues in a family group, even the family dog … "The ghosts at the haunted house!" she shouted.

Her father's eyes flicked over to her and back to the TV. "Shhh!"

"They must be a very professional ring of thieves," continued the journalist. "What plans do you have to protect the international art show scheduled for the Victoria Art Gallery next week? I understand the works expected will be worth millions of dollars."

"Yes, it is a very important show," agreed the chief. "But of course I cannot divulge our plans. Suffice it to say we have beefed up security at the gallery and will have extra officers on duty during the entire show."

"Thank you, Chief Carlson, and good luck."

"Don't wish him good luck!" Katie shrieked.

"Katie, can't you be quiet? I'm trying to hear the

news!" Her dad lifted one hand to run his fingers through his hair, and then, as if suddenly remembering how thin that hair really was, he scratched his forehead instead.

"I'm going to bed," Katie announced, and left the room.

She lay awake for hours thinking about the robberies and the old house and Chief Carlson. She was convinced the three were connected, but exactly how and why she had yet to figure out.

• • • • • •

Her room was too bright. Katie half opened her eyes, squinting against the sunlight, and then tossed back the covers and leapt out of bed. She threw on some clothes and ran up the stairs, two at a time, to the kitchen. An open newspaper was balanced in front of her mom's chair. A hand ventured out, felt around, landed on a mug of steaming coffee, picked it up and disappeared. Katie poured herself some orange juice and sat down.

"Good morning!" The paper crackled and her mom's soft brown eyes appeared around it. She smiled, and her eyes danced. "You had a nice long sleep."

"Not really." Katie wanted to ask her mom something but first needed to make sure her little brother wasn't listening. "Where's Michael?" she asked.

"He finished his breakfast and went outside to water his pumpkin patch. He's determined to grow a pumpkin big enough to climb inside, like Peter, Peter." Her mom laughed, then looked at Katie more closely. "How come you look so tired?"

"I couldn't get to sleep last night," Katie admitted, pouring cereal into her bowl and reaching for a banana.

"Something bothering you?" Her mom folded the newspaper and leaned her elbows on it, resting her chin on her hands. Sunlight slanted through the window, touching her short, curly brown hair and making it shine red-gold, but her eyes grew dark with concern.

"No. It's just … Mom, do you think a policeman could be a crook?"

Her mom's eyes widened in surprise, then they narrowed as she thought. "I'm sure it has been known to happen," she said. "Why?"

Katie shrugged. "Just wondering. What about the chief of police?"

"I guess so." Her mom frowned, thinking. After a minute she said, "In fact, I can't imagine a better job for a professional thief. He would know exactly where and when to strike and no one would suspect him."

"And," added Katie, "he could send the other police officers on wild ghos — er, wild goose chases so they'd never figure out what happened."

"Mmm." Her mother held the coffee mug in two hands in front of her chin. She took a sip, then tipped her head to one side, studying Katie's face. "You're up to something."

It wasn't really a question, yet it seemed to require an answer. Katie shoved an enormous spoonful of cereal into her mouth, so big she could barely breathe, much less talk. She hoped her mom would grow tired of watching her chew and return to the newspaper. The phone rang. Katie jumped out of her chair, chewing and gulping and attempting to swallow.

"Haow?"

There was a long silence, then a puzzled, "Katie?" Rusty's voice.

"Mm-mm."

"Sorry, I have the wrong number." Click.

"Who was that?" asked her mom as Katie returned to the table.

Katie swallowed the lump of cereal. "Wrong number."

Her mom picked up the paper as the phone rang again.

"Hello?"

"Katie, am I glad I got you! I was just talking to some real weirdo!"

"Oh?"

"Anyway, my dad says we could find all sorts of stuff about that house if we go to the library. Want to meet me there?"

"Okay, when?"

"This morning, 10:30 in the courtyard. Call Sheila. See you." Clunk. He was gone.

"Another wrong number?" her mother asked.

Katie shook her head as she sat down again. "It was Rusty. Can I meet him at the library this morning?"

"Really, Katie, I wish you wouldn't call him Rusty.

His name's Russell, and it's a very nice name. Or Russ — I think he prefers Russ now. But I know for sure he doesn't like Rusty."

"He likes it really, he just pretends not to. Besides, it suits him. He's got red hair and his last name is Gates. Rusty Gates. What's not to like?"

Katie's mom tried to look stern but ended up smiling. "His parents should have known better than to name him Russell," she said.

"So, can I go to the library?"

"Okay, I'll drop you off on my way to the office. How about taking Michael with you?"

"Aw, Mom …"

"I don't want to go anyway." Michael burst into the kitchen from the hall. "I'm going to Patrick's house."

"I thought you were outside!" Katie glared at her little brother. "I wish you would quit spying on me."

Michael's face fell. "I wasn't spying, I just came in and —"

"And lurked outside the door. Like I said — spying!"

· · · · · ·

Sheila and Rusty were sitting in the courtyard of the library when Katie arrived just after 10:30. They trooped inside and crossed the hushed room to the computer. Rusty sat down and started typing on the keyboard.

Katie grinned. "What are you looking up? Haunted?"

"How about ghosts?" asked Sheila.

"Or disappearances?" Katie chuckled.

Rusty ignored them both and whispered, "BC History."

He jotted down the call numbers of several books on the early history of Victoria. Then he darted across the room, stopped in front of a shelf, consulted his notes, scanned the books and took off in another direction. The girls trailed after him.

Finally he stopped. "Yes!" he said, and, reaching above his head, pulled down a book so heavy he staggered backward under its weight. He placed it on a table and the girls joined him as he flipped through it. There were sketches of the original Fort Victoria built by the Hudson's Bay Company in 1843. There were photographs of wooden buildings and muddy streets in the spring of 1858 when thousands of men arrived from San Francisco on their way to search for gold on the Fraser River.

Rusty found several more books on the early days of Victoria, and they flipped through them eagerly at first. But the stack of books grew higher and higher and still they had found no mention of a large house built on a lonely point of land by an unknown Englishman.

Katie spotted a book that interested her. It was all about shipwrecks on the coast of Vancouver Island. She tucked it under her arm.

"May I help you?"

She swung around and found herself looking into the friendly blue eyes of a woman the same height as herself.

The eyes sparkled with so much energy they made the woman seem as young as any of Katie's friends, even though her hair was gray and her skin lightly wrinkled.

"We're trying to find some information …" Katie began.

"On the haunted house!" Rusty interrupted.

Katie cringed, but the librarian did not laugh at them. Instead, she asked in a serious tone, "Which haunted house is that? There are several, you know."

"The old one on the waterfront," Katie told her. "Down on the point."

"Oh, you mean the old Matthews place," she nodded. "Yes, that one has quite a reputation. It seems to me," she added half to herself, tapping a finger against her forehead, "that there is just the one book …" She turned and strode across the room.

Scooping up a small stool, she carried it with her to a bookshelf, where she plunked it down, climbed onto it and reached up for a large, dark brown book with gold lettering. Stepping down, she sat on the stool and flipped the book open on her knees.

"Here it is," she said. "Built by Charles Matthews in 1861 and 1862. He returned to England to be married, and the couple lived in the house from September to November of 1862. English relatives of Elizabeth inherited it, but the house was never occupied again."

Katie gasped. Filling the page was a photograph of the old house when it was new. It gleamed under a fresh coat of paint, the grounds were neatly landscaped, and the sea sparkled in the background. Rusty's thin finger pointed at something to the left of the house.

A huge, fallen tree lay at the top of the bank. Katie felt a chill tingle across her scalp. Could it be the same one whose remains still lay there today?

"I remember when I was about your age," the librarian said, "we used to call it the haunted house, just like you do. I tried to talk my friends into going down there to peek in the windows — but they were always afraid."

"Did you ever go?" asked Katie.

"Just once, I crept up the stairs by myself and peeked in the window beside the front door. And the strange thing was, I was certain I saw something move in there. I ran away so fast that my friends took off before I reached them. I could never talk them into going anywhere near that house again."

Katie was fascinated. She wanted to ask more questions, but the librarian saw someone waiting at her desk and hurried away.

The three settled at a table and studied the book. It told of a storm during which Sir Charles Matthews disappeared and was presumed drowned. His body was never found. It mentioned a mystery surrounding the disappearance of his young wife, Elizabeth, some months later.

Sheila glanced at her watch. "It's almost noon!" She pushed back her chair and stood up.

"Yeah, I'm hungry." Rusty jumped to his feet.

Reluctantly, Katie closed the book and gave it to Rusty to check out, along with the one on shipwrecks.

They waited outside until he wandered out with his nose in the book. "Interesting," he muttered.

"What is?" asked Katie, taking the book on shipwrecks from him.

"Something about a bank robbery in 1864."

"What's that got to do with anything?"

"I don't know. It's just interesting."

He showed them a picture of an early Victoria bank. The caption under the photograph of the small wooden building explained that MacDonald's Bank was robbed of $30,000 on the night of September 22, 1864. The crime was never solved.

... six ...

Out To Lunch

"I'm off to the law courts," Sheila announced.

"What for?"

"To meet my mom. She forgot her lunch this morning."

"So?"

"So, when she phoned and I told her I was going to the library, she asked me to bring it. She can't buy lunch because she's broke, and anyway there's not enough time."

"What's she doing over there?" Rusty wanted to know.

"She has to testify in some case — police do that a lot, you know. Anyway, I gotta go. If I'm late, she won't have time to eat." Sheila started across the courtyard.

"Can I come?" asked Katie.

"Sure, if you hurry up!" Sheila called over her shoulder.

Katie looked uncertainly at Rusty. If she had to wait for him, there was no way she'd catch up with Sheila.

"I'll wait here," he said, heading for a bench. "I want to read this book."

"See you in a few minutes then," Katie said, and turned to run after Sheila.

Her friend had been swallowed up by a crowd of people that suddenly clogged the street as Katie headed for the provincial court building, across the street in the next block. She squeezed between a tall, thin couple and darted around a little boy holding his mother's hand; she tried to push past a very wide woman in a bright red dress, but couldn't find room with people coming the other way. Jumping up, she saw Sheila vanish behind a bulbous stomach in a green floral shirt. The man who belonged to the stomach had a sunburned scalp and little round sunglasses. He stood in the middle of the sidewalk, studying a map of Victoria and squinting up at the nearest street sign while the woman in the red dress rolled toward him.

Katie decided the best place for her was in the wake of the red dress as it pushed on around the green shirt. After that the crowd thinned, and Sheila was nowhere in sight. Katie broke into a run.

She reached the big square building and started up a long flight of stairs to the main entrance. Just before the first landing, she glanced up. She stopped abruptly. Two men stood at the top, two tall, strong-looking men, both with steel gray hair. The one facing Katie wore a police uniform. Her eyes flicked from him to the other man.

Confused, she walked up several more stairs until she could clearly see round, dark eyes under bushy eyebrows, a long, thin nose and wide, smiling lips. The other man wore a light gray, perfectly tailored suit, and even though his back was to her, Katie recognized him now. He started to turn. She fled.

"I'll see you here in an hour then, Spike," he called. "I have a lunch meeting."

The other man must be Spike Davis, one of the policemen Sheila's mom had told them about. Chief Carlson's footsteps clattered down the stairs behind her. She forced herself not to run — she did not want to attract his attention. At the bottom she turned to her left, hoping he would go the other way, toward the shops and restaurants of downtown Victoria. She continued walking away and then, hearing no one behind her, stopped and turned around. Chief Carlson was walking quickly in the opposite direction.

Katie studied his swiftly retreating back in his gray business suit — his long, purposeful strides, his arms swinging high — and knew she needed to follow him. She glanced up the now-empty stairs. "Come on, Sheila!" she whispered, and looked again toward Chief Carlson.

He had already reached the corner. Katie ran after him.

She crossed the street and followed him along the block. She slowed when he stopped at the next corner and turned to his left, waiting for the light to change. When it did, he crossed over and disappeared behind a

building while Katie ran for the corner. The light turned red. Traffic whizzed past. She craned her neck and jumped up, trying to see. There he was, striding head and shoulders above a group of elderly women. A van went by and blocked her view. It was followed by a delivery truck and then a bus. When the traffic cleared, the chief had vanished. She glanced back. Still no sign of Sheila.

The walk sign came on and Katie darted across the street. She was almost certain he was somewhere on this block because, unless he ran all the way, the chief had not had time to reach the next corner. She walked the length of the block, squinting in store windows, trying to see beyond her own reflection, knowing that whoever might be inside those stores could see her better than she could see them. She reached the end of the block and looked up and down the cross street — no sign of him.

Slowly retracing her steps, she tried to see into windows by rolling her eyes sideways, not turning her head. In the window of a small restaurant, a waitress wearing a yellow uniform was wiping a table. The waitress glanced up; Katie rolled her eyes forward.

She really should go back to the library. Sheila and Rusty would soon be wondering where she had gone. Katie hesitated, looked back along the block. Nothing. She turned away. And then she spotted Sheila, standing on the far corner, looking back and forth.

"Hey, Sheila!" She waved and called over the traffic noise, "Over here!"

Sheila crossed over to join her. "I saw you take off down the street," she said. "What are you doing? Where's Rusty?"

"Outside the library. He's busy reading, so he'll lose all track of time. Let's go!" Katie grabbed her wrist. "I'm following the chief."

"You are?" Sheila stared at a sidewalk cluttered with people walking in both directions. "How?"

"He's in one of these stores." Katie indicated with a sweep of her hand. "We just need to find out which one."

"Why?"

"We want to find out what he's up to."

"We do?"

"Yup." Katie stopped and pressed her nose against a shop window. A little boy licking a big ice cream cone looked up at her and blinked. She placed her hands beside her eyes, next to the glass, trying to make out the shadowy figures behind him.

"Who says he's up to anything?"

"I just know it. I get a feeling about these things."

"Oh yeah, 'Katie Reid, Private Investigator — With Feelings.'" Sheila yanked her away from the ice cream store. "He won't be in there. Mom says he's always on a diet. He likes to keep in shape."

"Sheila," Katie asked as they walked side by side, "does your mom like him? I mean, do they go out on dates or anything?"

Suddenly a hand grabbed Katie from behind and dragged her backward into the recess of a doorway. "Hey!" she yelled.

Hot, sticky fingers clamped tight over her mouth and nose. "Shut up," said a voice by her ear.

"What do you think you're doing?" Katie mumbled, trying to breathe.

"Didn't you see him?" Sheila whispered, releasing her hold.

"See who?"

"The chief! He's right there in the window."

Katie realized they were standing in the doorway of the small restaurant she had noticed earlier. "Lunchtime!" she said, and pulled Sheila inside.

"Please wait to be seated," read a white wooden sign on a short post just inside the door. A wall of white latticework formed a partition between the few tables near the window and others in the main part of the room.

The restaurant was crowded and bustling. There was no one in sight to seat them, so Katie squeezed in behind the sign and peeked between the small squares of the lattice. She gasped. The chief was sitting at the best table in the house, overlooking a window box filled with bright red geraniums and snowy white alyssum. His back was to her as he talked with two other men. One, dressed in a dark blue suit that pulled into tight little wrinkles across his stout back, faced the window. The top of his head gleamed in a shaft of sunlight, and he ran his chubby fingers over the smooth pink skin as though he were pushing back thick locks of hair. Opposite the chief was a slightly bigger, much younger man. His light brown hair curled over his forehead, his face was deeply tanned, and his plaid shirt fell open at the neck. He was devouring a big, juicy steak as if he had not eaten for days. Carlson picked away at a salad.

"How many in your party?"

Katie swung around. A middle-aged waitress in a faded yellow uniform stood with her hands on her hips, looking down with tired eyes. Sheila gazed wistfully out the glass door as though she was waiting for someone else and had no idea who Katie was.

"Three," Sheila answered without looking.

"Two," Katie said at the same time. She carefully wiped her finger across a board of the lattice divider and examined it as though she were a health inspector checking for cleanliness.

The waitress sighed and turned to Sheila. "Are you two together?"

"Why, yes." Katie waltzed over to Sheila. "It simply slipped my mind that our dear friend Russell will be joining us for luncheon."

Sheila rolled her eyes.

"Follow me," said the waitress, and led them to a freshly set table in the center of the room. They sat opposite each other; the waitress handed each of them a menu and placed another on the table. Then she hurried off to attend to her other customers.

"This is no good," Katie whispered, leaning forward. "We can't even see the chief's table."

Just then four women got up from a table right next to the lattice divider, directly behind the chief's table.

"Let's go," said Katie. She jumped up, grabbed two menus and hurried over. Settling into the chair, her back to the divider, she leaned backward and heard a rumble of voices behind her.

"This is ridiculous!" Sheila broke in. "Let's get out of here before that waitress comes back."

"No, I'm going to have pop and French fries — I've got enough money." Katie balanced one menu on her lap and opened the other to check the prices. The table was cluttered by half-empty coffee cups, a partially eaten piece of cream pie, and plates containing bits of lettuce, tomato, and pickles smeared with gobs of ketchup.

"Thought you'd left," the waitress grumbled, pushing a trolley to the table. "Something wrong with the other table?"

"Uh … too busy," Katie said. "Russell doesn't like to be out in the middle. He's a bit shy, you know. It's so much quieter over here."

"Is Russell a lot older than you?" The waitress looked hopeful.

"Uh, no, not really." Katie decided not to mention that he was younger.

"I'd better go find him." Sheila pushed away from the table and all but ran out of the restaurant.

The waitress handed a tall glass of ice water to Katie, then clattered all the dirty dishes into a bin. Katie, clutching the two large menus and the cold, slippery glass, watched her wipe the table with quick, angry strokes. The waitress rattled clean knives and forks together and reset the table, muttering to herself. When she strode away, Katie put down the glass and leaned as far back on her chair as she dared, raising the front legs off the floor.

"Get in and out fast," said a deep, rumbling voice that was cut off by a clatter of dishes from the kitchen.

A woman at a nearby table laughed, and as the sound died away Katie heard a softer voice say, "Not much time."

She leaned back just a little farther. Her chair teetered and threatened to fall backward and send her crashing into the latticework. She threw her weight forward. "Safely across the border," she heard the chief say just before the front legs of her chair hit the floor with a jolt and Sheila arrived with Rusty.

Before they could sit down, the waitress appeared and eyed Rusty with a disapproving look. "Ready to order?"

"I'll have a chocolate milkshake," said Sheila.

"That's all?"

"Yes."

The waitress picked up a little sign from the table and put it down again. Katie stared at it, wondering why she hadn't noticed it before. "You do realize there is a minimum charge at this time of day?"

"I'm sure we have that much," said Katie. Her hand slipped into her pocket, feeling for change.

"Each?"

"Time to go." Sheila turned and left, with Rusty close behind. Katie eased out of her chair. The waitress shook her head and picked up the glasses of ice water as Katie hurried away.

... seven ...

Art Lovers

"We need to follow them," Katie said when she joined the others outside.

Sheila groaned. "Who now?"

"The men with the chief, of course. We need to know who they are."

"Let's have some lunch first," Rusty suggested. "I'm hungry!"

"No! We've got to wait here until they come out. Besides, you're always hungry."

"I am not!"

"We can't just stand here looking stupid," Sheila pointed out.

"No. Okay, we'll walk slowly up the block, then back to the restaurant. They should be finished soon."

They walked to the corner, stopped and turned back. On the fourth trip, as they turned around just before reaching the restaurant, Rusty said, "Let's get ice cream cones."

"Good idea," Sheila agreed, reaching into her pocket and pulling out some change. "I can buy one and still have enough for bus fare."

Rusty counted his money. "I think I'll have licorice."

"But," Katie objected, "we're on the track of criminals here. Private investigators don't stop for ice cream cones!"

"Do you want one or not?" asked Sheila.

"Okay, peppermint chocolate chip. Rusty and I will wait here and stake out the place."

Rusty and Sheila exchanged glances. "Right," Sheila nodded. "You better stay here and keep an eye on her."

No sooner had Sheila gone than Rusty, glancing over his shoulder, asked, "Is that them?"

Katie turned. The plump man in the dark blue suit was walking toward them, talking to the much taller man in the plaid work shirt.

"Yes," she whispered. "Don't look! We have to follow them!"

"How do we follow them when they're behind us and we can't look?"

"I'll think of something." Katie glanced around. "Over here!" She grabbed Rusty's sleeve and pulled him to the nearest store. They looked in the window. "Try to seem interested," she said.

"Nice suit," said Rusty, looking at the dark, pin-striped men's suit displayed in the window. "Do you think I should try it on?"

"Funny," said Katie, and glanced down the street.

"They got into a car," she whispered. "A big white convertible. They're going to pass us in a minute. Don't look."

Rusty turned his head. Katie tossed back her curls and gazed into the shop window. In it she could clearly see the road behind her. The car rolled past. The plump man was driving, his bald head gleaming like a bowling ball. The other man leaned back lazily in the sunshine.

"Ice cream, anyone?"

Katie jumped. She took her cone from Sheila and they started up the street, licking their ice cream.

"So, we meet again." All three swung around at once. Chief Carlson smiled, a wide smile filled with gleaming white teeth. "I wish I could still eat ice cream." He patted his flat stomach and strode past them.

They stared after him.

"Well, there's only one thing left to do," said Katie.

"Yeah," Rusty agreed. "Go to your place and get some lunch."

"Not yet. First, we go to the art gallery."

"Why should we go to the art gallery?"

"To check it out. We've got to stop the robbery."

"What robbery?"

Katie explained about the news story and told them about the conversation she had overheard. "I just know Chief Carlson and his buddies are planning to rob the art gallery."

Rusty looked at Sheila and raised his eyebrows. Sheila rolled her eyes.

"Then why don't you go and tell the police?" Rusty asked.

"Right. Do you think they'd believe a kid who walked in off the street and told them the big boss was planning a major burglary? You don't even believe me, and you're my partners."

"You're right," Sheila agreed. "They'd fall over laughing."

"That's why we need evidence. Let's go."

. . . . . .

Twenty minutes later they got off the bus at the north end of Moss Street and walked a half-block to the Art Gallery of Greater Victoria. Even though it was only a few blocks from her house, Katie had never been inside the gallery. It was a low, cement building set back from the road under stately Garry oaks. A strip of brown bricks ran the length of the front beneath high, narrow windows. Behind this newer section was the original building, a huge mansion with a cupola on the roof.

"That house was built back in 1889," Rusty told them, eager to show off his new-found knowledge. "They had an orchard and tennis courts here and even a coach house and stables!"

Katie had other things on her mind. She watched their reflections walk toward them in the long glass wall as the three went up the wide, cement stairs to the main entrance. Something caught her eye. In the parking lot behind her was a long, white convertible.

Inside, they found themselves in a large, impersonal foyer. At a desk to the right sat a young woman with very short brown hair and gobs of makeup. She was chatting with a good-looking young man. The three walked up to her desk and stood there, waiting. The couple ignored them.

Katie cleared her throat.

The young woman stopped talking, turned and peered down her long, thin nose. "Can I help you?" she asked, tight-lipped and angry.

Katie stared at her dark purple lips and mauve eyelids and wondered if she had been in a bad accident. "We just want to look at the art," she said. "We happen to be art lovers."

The purple lips parted. "You do realize there is an admission fee?"

The silence lengthened. The young woman's eyes narrowed until Katie began to wonder if her gooey black eyelashes had stuck together permanently. "Of course we know," she replied.

Pondering what to do next, Katie let her gaze wander into the bright, airy room to her left. Graceful sculptures stood on tall pedestals against a curving wall: a powerful whale; a graceful seabird; a beautiful, fluid, circular figure in pure white marble that somehow made her think of peace … Katie's eyes widened. Behind the figure stood a short, plump man in a dark blue suit that pulled into tight wrinkles across his back. He was staring at something near the ceiling, and as he did, the top of his head gleamed in the light. When he wandered out of sight, it was all Katie could do to keep from chasing after him. "What we really came for," she said, "is to speak to the manager."

"I see. And I assume you have an appointment with the *director?*" The receptionist stared stonily at Katie, then made a show of scanning the appointment book.

"No. Actually, we have some very important information for him."

"About a robbery," Rusty added.

"This is not the police station," the receptionist snapped. Her fingernails tapped against the desk, a scratchy, irritating sound that sent a chill down Katie's back.

"Now, if you don't mind …" The receptionist turned her back on them and looked up at the young man, who leaned against the wall, arms crossed, an amused smile on his handsome face. "I have work to do," she said.

"Don't you think we know where we are?" Katie asked. "The robbery is going to be here — and soon. We have inside information. If you don't let us talk to the — uh — *director,* the robbery will be your fault."

"Oh, all right!" The receptionist slammed down her pen and pushed her chair back from the desk. "I'll go ask him to talk to you. It's probably the only way to get rid of you."

The young man wandered into the next room,

"What are we going to tell him?" Rusty whispered.

"Only that one of the robbers is here right now, checking out the alarm system."

"You mean one of the men from the restaurant?" Rusty backed a few steps toward the exit.

Katie nodded. "The fat one," she said.

"He followed us!"

"How could he have? He was here when we got here." Katie shook her head. "No, he must have come to study the layout and the security system. And that proves we're on the right track."

The receptionist returned. "Mr. Anderson will see you." She looked around and, seeing the young man had gone, glared down at them. "Follow me."

She led them to a large, bright room with long windows and thick, creamy carpeting. Katie stopped in her tracks. Sheila continued toward the desk. Rusty was nowhere in sight.

"You wanted to see me?" The director stopped writing and looked up at them. He removed his glasses from his chubby, round face and smiled uncertainly. His bald head shone in the light from the window; his dark suit pulled into tight wrinkles around the tops of his arms and blended with the rich blue of the drapes. Sheila turned to Katie, expecting her to do the talking.

"Yes," said Katie, stepping boldly forward to stand beside her friend. "We just wanted to say that we like your art gallery and we, uh, we think it's too bad people have to pay to see it."

Sheila's eyebrows raised. Mr. Anderson frowned, rubbing his chubby fingers across his chin.

"Miss Kirk mentioned something about a robbery?"

"Yes." Sheila took a step forward. "You see, Katie thinks …"

"Yes. I think — we all think it's highway robbery that kids like us, true art lovers, are forced to pay simply to look at the art," Katie said hastily. "And now —" she grabbed Sheila by the arm and dragged her toward the door "— we really must be going."

• • • • • •

Rusty waited outside on the grass beneath an oak tree. "Well?" he said as they met in the parking lot.

"It's him, the director. Mr. Anderson is in on it. He's helping the chief rob the gallery!"

"Let me get this straight," said Rusty. "You think the chief of police and the director of the art gallery are both crooks?"

Katie nodded. They reached the sidewalk and started down Moss Street toward Katie's house. "It all fits. There's no other explanation."

"Except one," said Sheila.

"What?"

"Who else would Chief Carlson meet with to plan security for the gallery? They said there isn't much time, which there isn't — the big art show is next week. And when the chief said, 'Safely across the border,' he probably meant they would all be glad when the art moved on to Seattle and it wasn't their responsibility any more."

"No, but …" Katie's heart sank. Sheila could be right.

"But what about that other man? Who's he? If you ask me, he looks like a criminal."

"Maybe he owns a security firm," suggested Rusty. "And I've been thinking. You know those two cops that go down to the house all the time?"

Sheila nodded. "Spike Davis and Archie McFee?"

"Yeah. If there's something going on there, I bet they're the ones doing it."

Sheila grinned. "Come to think of it, Spike looks a little like Carlson. Same size, same coloring, about the same age. Maybe it was him we saw through the window."

Katie pictured the man she had seen talking with Chief Carlson at the law courts in the full light of day. She thought of the dim interior of the old house. And she didn't say another word.

· · · · · ·

When his mom picked him up late that afternoon, Rusty took along the book about early houses and buildings in Victoria, and left the one on shipwrecks for Katie. She carried the book and a glass of iced tea to the backyard, settled on a lounge chair and opened the book. At the front was a map of Vancouver Island. All along the coast were little black silhouettes of three-masted sailing ships, their bows pointing skyward, their sterns underwater. Each one represented a shipwreck. There were dozens of them on the rocky, storm-ridden west coast of the island, but very few on the inner, protected eastern coast-line. Katie sat up straighter — one of them was on a shoal just east of Foul Bay. Yes! It was just off the very point of land where the old house stood. Katie was sure of it.

Excitedly, she flipped through the book, searching for more detailed information, which was not easy to find because each shipwreck was listed according to the year it went down, not its location. When at last she found what she was looking for, Katie settled back to read.

The shipwreck, she discovered, was unconfirmed but believed to have been a Spanish sailing vessel that had been raiding Native villages and British ships along the coast. The author suggested that because the ship's hold was full of illegally taken goods, the Spanish ship would have avoided the Hudson's Bay Company's trading post at Fort Victoria, which would explain why there was no definite record of its disappearance.

The local Natives claimed the ship hit a shoal and sank during a stormy night in 1857. No trace was ever found. Local authorities suspected that if a ship had hit the shoal, it must have somehow caught fire and burned to the waterline before sinking, because the water was too shallow to cover a ship of that size.

What this long-ago event had to do with the mysterious happenings at the house this summer, Katie had no idea, but she felt certain there was a link and was determined to find it.

... eight ...

Words from the Past

Katie propped her bike against the side of Sheila's house and plodded around to the back. And there was Sheila, standing in the middle of her yard with her back to Katie, head bent and feet slightly apart. Suddenly she twisted sideways, swung a club and sent a small white ball sailing neatly over the fence into her neighbor's yard. It made a loud clunk as it landed. Sheila's shoulders tensed. There was another clunk, a dog yelped, then everything was quiet.

"What are you doing?" Katie demanded.

Sheila glanced over her shoulder. "Practicing."

"Practicing for what? And why?"

"My mom and I are learning golf so we can play together." She swung at a daisy, missed and sent bits of grass flying. "At least, we were," she added gloomily.

"What do you mean 'were'?"

"Oh, nothing. It's just — nothing." Sheila stared down at her golf club.

"Just what? Sheila, you can tell me. Am I your best friend, or what?"

"Oh — she's gone golfing with that stupid Chief Carlson, that's all."

"Golfing? With Carlson? Is that like, I mean, a date?"

"No, it's not like a date!" Sheila snapped.

"But — does she go *out* with him? Does she *like* him?"

"How should I know? Just forget it, okay? I knew I shouldn't tell you — you never stop asking questions!" Sheila dropped the club and stormed across the grass, up the steps and into the house. The screen door slammed behind her.

Katie stared at the closed door. Sheila angry? No, couldn't be. Sheila never got angry, never lost her cool. Not Sheila.

"What's going on?"

Katie jumped at the voice right behind her. She swung around and narrowed her eyes. "What are you doing here?"

Rusty stood just inside the fence, holding a folded sheet of paper in one hand. His brow furrowed and he stared accusingly at Katie. "I heard yelling. What did you do to Sheila?"

"Me? I didn't do anything! She's the one that was yelling!"

Rusty didn't believe her; Katie could see that in his eyes. He opened his mouth to say something, but Katie quickly changed the subject. "What's that?"

He glanced down at the paper. His face lit up. "Guess where I've been?"

"I don't know. And I don't really care either."

"At the archives."

"Wow, that sure sounds exciting."

"Well, it just so happens, it was. My dad helped me find some old books and pictures and stuff that Charles and Elizabeth Matthews left behind. Most of it was boring, but just when he was putting it away, a folded piece of paper fell to the floor. I picked it up, and after we read it Dad let me make a copy. Guess what it is?"

Katie grinned. "A bill from Ghost Busters?"

"Ha, ha! No, it just happens to be a letter to Elizabeth from her sister in England. Only Elizabeth never read it because she disappeared before it got here."

The screen door creaked open and Sheila stepped out. She settled on the top step. "Read it," she said.

Rusty looked from one to the other. He shook his head and glared at Katie accusingly. Then he unfolded the paper and began to read.

My Dearest Sister:

I have just this day received your letter and felt the need to reply immediately.

It must be horrid for you to live in such a wild country. I myself would be terrified upon hearing such unsettling stories about the house in which I lived.

How can you speak so calmly about noises beneath the floorboards of your home? I pray you will take the advice of Carlson, your butler. He sounds to be a wise man. Wherever did you find him in such a barbaric land?

Knowing you, I expect you will already have decided to explore the underground tunnel you discovered at the beach.

What if it does lead to a cave beneath your house? That does not disprove the ghosts. Such a cave could be occupied by the tortured spirits of all the poor souls who have met with violent death on the spot.

I beg you not to go in there!

Yes, I do recall the cave we discovered when we were children. How could I ever forget? I was petrified every second that you forced me to spend in there. Do you not remember the rats? If it is not spirits making the noises beneath your house, then it is most likely rats.

Lizzie, you were always the adventurous member of our family. I often think that you would have been far happier had you been a man. It is so much easier for a man to satisfy his hunger for adventure in this society of ours!

At least you have been able to escape the England you find so tedious. You will share in creating a brand-new colony. Such a life must be both exciting and frightening.

As for myself, I could never simply pick up and leave all my family and friends, perhaps forever. Especially to live with a man I did not love.

I pray this letter finds you well and safe.

Your loving sister,
Mary

"Wow," whispered Sheila. "Poor Mary!"

"Poor Elizabeth, you mean. She's the one who disappeared," Katie said.

"Did you notice the butler's name?" asked Rusty, folding the letter.

Katie nodded. "Carlson. What a coincidence!" She looked up at Sheila, who still sat on the step, elbows resting on her knees. "Do you think they're related?"

"How should I know?" Sheila stood, clomped down the stairs, picked up the golf club and started swinging it back and forth, swishing over the long grass.

"Your mom likes him, doesn't she?" asked Rusty.

"Who knows?"

"Does she go out with him?"

"None of your business!" The club swung faster.

Rusty's mouth dropped open. He snapped it closed and glanced at his watch. "I gotta go now, I'm catching the bus to meet Mom at work. I just stopped by to show you this." He put the paper into his knapsack, turned on his heel and was gone.

"You hurt his feelings," Katie said quietly.

"Mmm. As if you could care."

"I think he likes you."

"Huh?"

"Rusty. I think he likes you."

"Well, he's okay. I like him too."

"No. I mean he *likes* you."

"Oh, *please*! Your cousin Rusty? No way."

"Well anyway, he might be a really nice guy."

"Rusty?"

"No. Well, he's okay — for a cousin. But I meant Chief Carlson. We don't know, but he might be a nice guy"

"Forget it!" Sheila swung so hard at a daisy that a solid chunk of grass and earth flew out, leaving a deep hole in the lawn. But Sheila didn't stop. She swung viciously at the little white daisies as if she hated the very sight of them.

This was too weird. Nothing ever bothered Sheila — she was the best-natured person in the world. Something had to be done. "Let's go look for that tunnel," Katie suggested.

Sheila paused with the club raised over her head. "Okay. Why not? Wait while I write a note for my mother — as if she cared."

"Sheila!"

But Sheila just walked away, her shoulders squared, clutching the golf club in a fierce grip.

• • • • • •

The girls hid their bikes under some broom bushes and stared up at the old house. "Where do we start?" asked Sheila.

"I don't know. Let's try the side where the little inlet is."

They clambered down to the beach and walked along it, carefully studying the bank beside them. It was made of clay, with the occasional rock or a clump of bushes.

Katie scrambled partway up the bank and clung precariously to a broom bush while she examined the solid wall of clay behind it.

"Come here!" Sheila cried, and Katie slid down. She found her friend near the wharf, standing on the beach with her hands on her hips, eyes riveted on a large boulder embedded in the bank.

"What?" Katie asked.

"See it?"

"See what?"

Sheila walked to the base of the boulder. She reached up and rubbed it with her fingertips. "Remember the mammoth?"

"How old do you think I am, anyway?"

Sheila glanced over her shoulder, frowning. "I mean the one at the museum."

Katie thought back to a rainy day last winter when their teacher had taken them to the Royal British Columbia Museum. "Yeah. It's huge. So what?"

"Remember the display around it?"

"Sure, fake snow and big rocks that look real. You had to touch them to tell they were made out of fiberglass ... Hey!"

Sheila was working her fingers around the bottom edge of the boulder, examining the crack between it and the clay bank. "Hey what?"

"They're really light, hollow or something." Katie stood on tiptoe on a rock and reached up to rub her fingertips over the boulder. It felt strangely smooth and curiously unrocklike. She tapped it with her knuckles and listened. Did it sound hollow?

"Mm-hmm," said Sheila. "Get me a strong stick with a pointy end."

Katie set off in search of a stick. Maybe Sheila was right. Maybe the boulder was not really a boulder at all but a cleverly disguised door into the tunnel. Katie was excited but, at the same time, wished she had been the one to notice it first. She found a stout stick and ran back with it. Sheila, clinging by her toes to a narrow ledge, took the stick and forced the pointed end into the crack beside the boulder. She pushed the other end toward the bank. The stick bent as though it would break.

"Get another stick!"

When Katie came back they wedged both sticks into the narrow space. They pushed. The levers creaked. Nothing moved. They reset the levers, working them further in behind the boulder. They pushed again.

"It moved!" said Sheila.

"I didn't see anything."

"No, but it creaked, I'm sure of it. Try again."

This time there was an unmistakable creak and the boulder inched forward. They dropped the sticks and worked their fingers behind the boulder's edge. With a deep groan of protest it swung open. They stared in surprise. It was a heavy, hinged door, the outside shaped to look exactly like a large rock.

The girls now gazed into a dark hole. Katie scrambled inside. "Come on. Let's see where it goes."

... nine ...

The Cave

"It sure is dark in there." Sheila hung back at the entrance.

"What did you expect, a skylight? Let's go."

The air was cool as they felt their way along the walls of the tunnel, walking single file because it was not quite wide enough to walk side by side. The sunlight at the entrance behind them provided the only source of light.

"I thought you always had your flashlight in your knapsack," whispered Sheila.

"I do," Katie whispered back. "We're all supposed to, remember? It's part of our kit." She sighed. This had been her one chance to prove to Sheila the importance of having an official investigator's kit, and she had blown it. "But I forgot my knapsack at home today."

Gradually, as their eyes became accustomed to the dim light, they could make out the curving roof of the tunnel above their heads. It was shored up with huge

timbers used as posts and crossbeams.

The tunnel soon widened into a large cave. They felt, rather than saw, the ceiling far above their heads. The only sound was the hollow echo of their footsteps bouncing off rock walls. Katie pointed to the opposite side of the cave, where she could just see the dim outline of a stairway, painted white. They crept toward it, scarcely daring to breathe.

Closer now, they could see stairs disappearing into the darkness above. At the bottom was a post with a nail sticking out of it, and hanging on the nail was a large, white, plastic flashlight.

Katie reached for it. But just as her hand touched the cool plastic, a loud thump hammered through the cave, echoing off the walls and ceiling. She jumped back. The sound stopped. A man's voice surrounded them, seeming to come from all directions at once. A pinpoint of light glimmered at the top of the stairs.

The girls held their breath. The voice was more distinct now, coming from up above.

"Come here and give me a hand!"

Another, more distant voice gave a muffled reply.

Katie climbed up Sheila's heels as they raced for the tunnel, stumbling over loose rocks. At the far end, a ray of sunlight beckoned to them. Voices echoed around them. Sheila had almost reached the exit when Katie's foot slipped between two rocks and caught. She stumbled and fell heavily. There was a loud creak from behind. Footsteps started down the stairs.

Katie's foot was firmly stuck, wedged between two rocks. She twisted around and pulled at it with both hands, but it wouldn't come free.

A voice called something unintelligible; the footsteps stopped.

For once, Katie was happy to see that her shoelace had come undone. She twisted her foot to work it loose, out of the shoe. That done, she yanked on the empty shoe. It pulled free so suddenly, Katie tumbled backward. Scrambling to her feet, ready to run, she noticed the square corner of something just visible under the rock, which had moved slightly to free her shoe. Digging furiously at the rocks around it, she grabbed the protruding corner and pulled. The object came free and she ran for the entrance, not even feeling the rough rocks under her sock, aware only of heavy footsteps thudding down the stairs behind her.

She burst out into blinding sunlight. Sheila pushed the fake boulder into place and they scrambled up the bank, Katie stumbling behind Sheila, scarcely able to see where she was going in the sun's glare, clutching her shoe in one hand and the small package in the other.

Reaching the top, Katie stopped to shove her foot into her shoe. She stuffed the package into the big front pocket of her shorts, and the two girls ran side by side to retrieve their bikes. Yanking her bike free of the bushes, Katie glanced toward the house, hoping that no one inside was looking out. To the left of the building was a pile of leafy branches, looking as if it had just recently been stacked, waiting for a bonfire. She tapped Sheila on the shoulder and pointed. Sheila looked, gasped, jumped on her bike and took off up Rotten Road. Katie was not far behind. As they passed closer to the stack, she glanced sideways and caught a glimpse of silver metal. She pedaled faster.

"I need to tie up my shoelace," Katie called, just before Sheila turned onto the paved road at the top of the hill. Sheila stopped and waited for her. Katie had just straightened up, ready to go, when they heard it. The powerful roar of a car engine starting up. It came from below them, at the bottom of Rotten Road.

Sheila's eyes widened. Katie's heart raced. "Do you think they saw us?"

"Don't know. Let's get out of here — to your house!"

There were several residential roads leading back up to the main road that wound its way peacefully along Victoria's waterfront. Faced with a choice of turning left or right, Sheila did not hesitate. She turned left. The engine sound grew louder behind them as they sped away. Sheila turned left again, back toward the water, onto a short no-through road. Katie was not far behind. They stopped and pulled in under the low branches of a cedar. The car roared to the top of Rotten Road, zoomed ahead, turned left and whipped past the road they were hiding on.

"Let's go!" said Sheila as the engine sound retreated up the hill in front of them.

Afraid the car would come back at any minute, looking for them, they reached the main road and cut down the first side street, away from the waterfront. Every time a car came up behind them they kept their heads down and pedaled even harder than before.

They zigzagged their way along a network of residential streets until they reached the foot of St. Charles. There they turned right and started up the steep hill. Katie had never gone up that hill so fast in her life. Her legs pumped like pistons, her front wheel close behind Sheila's back one. They reached Rockland Avenue and didn't slow down until they turned into Katie's driveway. They hid their bikes around the back, slammed through the downstairs door and collapsed, exhausted, in Katie's bedroom.

"Whoa!" said Sheila. "We made it! I thought we were goners for sure!"

"Can you believe that cave?" Katie paused to catch her breath. "It's so huge — and it must be right under the house!"

"Yeah," Sheila said. "I can't believe no one knows about it!"

"Someone does," Katie reminded her.

As they talked, they heard footsteps crashing down the stairs. Michael peeked around the half-closed door. Sheila was sprawled on the chair, her legs stretched out in front of her, her head thrown back and her arms flung out sideways. Katie lay collapsed on the bed; her heart beat quick and hard against her ribs.

"What happened to you?" Michael demanded. "How come your faces are all red, like big fat rock crabs?"

"Go away!" Katie yelled. She hated the way he poked his nose into everything she did.

Michael moved out of sight. Everything was quiet. Then they heard a thin, squeaky voice just outside the door. *"Row, row, row your boat ..."*

Katie had never liked that song, and Michael knew it. She got up and slammed the door. "Go away, Michael," she said. "Can't you tell we're busy?"

Katie flopped back onto the bed and sank into the soft mattress. She would not move a muscle for the rest of the day. Her legs felt like lead, heavy and lifeless; her skin was hot and drenched with perspiration.

After what seemed like a long time, she began to cool down, become comfortable. Soon after that, her damp skin turned cold and she started to shiver. She sat up and reached for the folded blanket at the end of her bed. That's when she felt the package still in her pocket. She pulled it out.

Sheila watched with interest as Katie turned the small, square package over in her hands. She gently removed the wrapping, examining it carefully, rubbing it between her fingers. She had never seen anything like it before, a strange kind of shiny, waterproof material, not plastic, but sort of rubbery. It was cracked with age. Inside was a thin book, just slightly larger than the paperback mysteries Katie loved to read. It was bound in brown leather, soft and supple.

The book flopped open on her lap. Its thin pages were yellowed with time, especially toward the outer edges, and they felt crisp under her fingers, like the skin of an onion. Each page was covered with neat but scratchy handwriting, the thickness of each letter uneven. Sheila moved from the chair to sit beside Katie. They read the title page: *The Diary of Elizabeth Matthews, October 1862 to June 1863.*

"That's odd," said Katie. "I thought she disappeared the first winter she was here."

"Me too," Sheila agreed.

Near the middle of the book, a narrow piece of paper served as a bookmark. Katie turned to it and found, to her surprise, a second title page. The handwriting in this section was messy, and the words big and bold. There were several ink smudges on the page, as if the writer had been in a hurry. This inscription read: *Diary of Eliza Carlson, 1863 —.*

"I wonder who Eliza Carlson was? Do you think she could be Chief Carlson's great-grandmother or something? I wonder what happened to Elizabeth Matthews? Hey! I bet Eliza was the butler's wife and the two of them got rid of Elizabeth so they could have the house and everything. Maybe Carlson's whole family have been thieves and murderers from way back! Maybe …" Katie glanced at Sheila's white face and broke off.

Sheila turned away. "Are you finished?"

"Sure. Okay. You know what? I bet Chief Carlson has nothing to do with this. You're probably right: the chief and the director met to plan security at the art gallery. And maybe it wasn't even him we saw in the house

— we only caught a glimpse of him, and it was kind of dark and all."

Sheila didn't answer.

Katie closed the book. "Sheila, what's wrong? Don't you like him?"

Sheila's face went from white to bright pink. "I just don't like the way he always hangs around my mother these days." She put her hand to her forehead. "He's so old and … slimy! He must be at least fifty!"

"That's not so bad. My dad's forty-three and he still plays tennis and everything. He even water-skis!"

"I just don't like him, okay? And what if we find out he's a crook? Or worse? My mother will never forgive me."

Katie hesitated. She ran her fingers through her hair, thinking. "It's probably just a coincidence," she said. "I bet Eliza Carlson has nothing to do with Chief Carlson. I mean, Carlson's kind of a common name. I think. Isn't it?" Katie felt like biting her own tongue. Why couldn't she stop babbling?

"I've got to go." Sheila slid off the bed. She walked across the room, shoulders stiff, fists clenched at her sides, and pulled open the door.

Katie stared after her, almost afraid to open her mouth in case she said something dumb. "Want to do something tomorrow?" she heard herself say.

Sheila shook her head. "It's Mom's day off. We're going to the beach." And she was gone.

Katie lay back and studied the white plaster ceiling.

Sometimes she envied Sheila. Her friend's mom always had time to spend with her, alone. They did all sorts of stuff together, like hiking and swimming and playing golf. Sheila even went to the gym with her mom to do weight training. No wonder she was so good at sports.

If only Katie's own parents had been content with just one child …

... ten ...

The Diary

October 13, 1862

There is nothing to do in this wretched country. It has rained for three days and three nights. Everything is wet.

Victoria is a horrid little town with streets of knee-deep mud. It is clogged with ragged, dirty prospectors who have returned from the gold fields up north in the Cariboo, most of them poorer than when they left. All around the town, they live in wretched tents, too poor to book passage south to San Francisco or return to their homes. The men intend to spend the winter here where the weather is mild. Come spring they will return by pack train or wagon to the newly discovered gold fields in Richfield and Barkerville, where they will try their luck again.

The few British ladies who have settled here are more boring than their poor husbands, many of whom are under contract to work for the Hudson's Bay

Company. If they were looking for a better life, they have been bitterly disappointed. I may as well be in England for all the excitement I have found here.

I have decided to write a diary as something to pass the time. I shall begin by telling of my trip over to this little colony.

We traveled across the Atlantic in a comfortable steamship. The trip was pleasant enough, and at first our fellow passengers were good company. However, only a few days out, we were beset by storms. The constant rocking of the ship kept most of them from the table.

Charles was among those stricken. He kept to our cabin and took on a rather greenish hue. I brought him dry biscuits and weak tea, which he sometimes was able to swallow.

I never once felt seasick. Surely I was born to spend my life upon the sea! I love it all: the creaking of the ship as she climbs over mountainous waves; the endless horizons of gray water flecked with white foam; the salt-laden wind and the cool spray upon my face. I felt alive as never before.

The captain and I enjoyed many meals alone. The other passengers and crew were either too sick or too busy to join us. He entertained me with exciting stories of high adventure on the seas. He told me of visits to colorful ports both large and small all around the world. These places I can only long to visit.

Such folly to have been born a woman!

We disembarked in the heat of a tropical sun at Colon. There we climbed aboard a funny little train that chugged though the jungle, carrying us overland to Panama City and the Pacific Ocean.

The inescapable heat, the mosquitoes which constantly fly in one's eyes and whine in one's ears, the unfamiliar food, and the sickly brown water combined to make many travelers ill.

Charles was one of the worst. I had great trouble being sympathetic toward him while he moaned and complained as if he were a spoiled child. Yet I had to care for him as patiently as a mother, putting my own feelings aside. His clothes hung loose around his middle by that time, and the lovely ruby ring I gave him as a wedding gift slipped easily off his finger. Even so, he remained a portly man.

— The rain has finally stopped! The sun is breaking through the clouds and making the sea sparkle. I am going to take a walk on the beach.

Katie placed the diary face down on her stomach. She was propped up comfortably against pillows and now put her head back to think. She felt sorry for Elizabeth Matthews. Katie couldn't imagine leaving her family behind and setting off for a new, primitive world where she would be stuck in a lonely mansion with a husband she didn't love.

Picking up the diary, she read on eagerly.

October 17, 1862
I have not found time to write for several days because Charles invited guests who recently arrived from England. Of course I had to entertain them with cards

and silly games and senseless conversation. I also had to supervise the preparation of meals. Speaking of which, Charles eats enough for any three people and has developed a great, fat belly. His fingers are so plump now, his ruby ring digs deeply into the flesh.

There appears to be some small problem in the kitchen. The cook, the houseboy, and a maid all reported hearing strange noises from underneath the floor. They were frightened and threatened to leave but were eventually soothed by our wonderful butler, Carlson. He told them a wild story of the tragic deaths of many Spanish seamen along with two old Indian men. Then he explained that the story was most likely untrue and so they should not believe it. Even if it were true, he said, no one should worry about ghosts, as he did not believe in them.

The maid was quite charmed by his manner. He is a dark, good-looking man who could pass as a Spaniard himself. He has a devastating smile which reveals a row of very white teeth and an enchanting dimple in his right cheek. The Chinese cook and houseboy also chose to ignore the foolish tales of tortured spirits haunting the ground beneath our house. However, it seems to me that if Carlson had not told them of it, there would have been no need to charm them into disbelieving it.

Nevertheless, everything is settled now. The servants stayed on and the guests have at last continued on their way. Now I can continue my tale.

We spent almost a week in Panama City, during which time Charles made up for all the meals he had missed. Then we boarded a steamship that would carry us up the Pacific Coast. This one was smaller and much less comfortable than the first. It was overcrowded with men arriving from all parts of the world, hoping to make their fortunes in gold. I expect they too will be living in tents before long. Now is not the time to continue north to the Cariboo, where the snow will soon be falling and the ground freezing over.

The Pacific Ocean did not live up to its name, as we did not have one calm day on the entire journey. All the passengers, save myself, were very ill. I felt sorry for Charles. If only he would not carry on so!

We changed ships at San Francisco, where even more men came aboard, seeking riches beyond imagining. California's own gold rush ended some years ago, which left many prospectors searching for a new hope of becoming rich.

At last we arrived at Esquimalt Harbor on September 15, a warm and sunny day. I longed to let Charles disembark alone. Unfortunately, this was not possible.

— God save us! Charles has just now arrived home and discovered some sort of disturbance in the kitchen. I must go and intervene before he causes all our servants to quit.

If only Charles were more like Carlson!

Katie skimmed through several pages of boring notes and observations. She discovered more and more references to noises scaring the staff. The entry for November 23rd caught her interest:

Most of the servants have left us now. Carlson stays and continues to be very kind. I do not know how I would have managed these last months without him. He is much more than a butler — he is a good friend.

I have sent a letter to my sister telling her of the exciting discovery I made on the beach yesterday. Just at dusk, as I was returning from my walk, I bent to pick up a brightly colored shell. The wind was gusting when I happened to glance up toward the bank where a broom bush was swaying in the breeze. Behind it, I caught a brief glimpse of movement — a small animal, perhaps, or a bird.

I moved closer to investigate. Working my way behind the thick bush I discovered a hole large enough to squeeze through. Just inside was a big, round rock that looked as though it would completely fill the hole if it were rolled into place.

Darkness was falling and I could not see much beyond the entrance, but I stuck my head inside and called. My voice echoed so hollowly that I imagined a long tunnel of some sort. It appears to lead in the direction of the house.

Perhaps there are some animals in there, or even people, such as prospectors who have run out of money and are living in the tunnel beneath our kitchen. I should think it would be drier and far more comfortable than those miserable tents! At the same time it might explain the strange noises. Last night I told Carlson about the cave and he advised me to stay away. He thinks it may be dangerous.

I intend to investigate as soon as the wild storm

that is raging around the house has blown itself out. The tide is extremely high and the wind funneling into the inlet is blowing spray completely over the bank. It would not be possible to make my way down there today.

I will not tell Charles of my discovery because he would forbid me to explore it, but if I tell Carlson I am determined to explore the tunnel with or without his help, I am hoping he will choose to accompany me. I am slightly nervous about going alone, but if need be, that is exactly what I shall do.

After this entry there were several blank pages. Katie turned them gently.

The next entry was dated February of 1863. Katie felt the hair bristle on the back of her neck. This was after Elizabeth was supposed to have disappeared. She could hardly wait to read more.

"Katie! Come and help get dinner ready!" her mother called.

Katie glared up at the ceiling, then skimmed over the next few pages. The name Frank Carlson jumped out at her, and something to do with Elizabeth living beneath her own house.

"Katie!"

"I'm coming!" She closed the diary and hid it under her pillow.

... eleven ...

Eliza

It was much later before Katie got back to her room. She closed her door, pulled the diary from under her pillow and turned to the 1863 entry.

February 1863
I don't know the exact date, as I've been out of touch for so long now.

After more than three months, I finally explored the tunnel. I am now living underneath the house that once was my unhappy home. What's more, Frank has been living here for most of four years!

There is a large, surprisingly dry cave down here. We have moved some of the furniture from the house above and made it quite livable. That is how I found my diary, tucked away safely in a drawer of my dressing table.

No one dares to come near the house now, not after the tragic night of November 23rd.

The wind howled that night as I lay in my bed. Waves pounded against the shore. Then, over the raging wind, I heard a faint cry. It was repeated several times. I got up and went to find Charles. He had heard it too, and, fearing that someone was hurt and calling for help, he determined to go out and investigate.

I pleaded with him to take Carlson along, but, being Charles, he ignored my advice. I sat in my room, listening to the pitiful cries until suddenly I heard a fearful scream. Certain that it was Charles, I ran outside in my nightgown, foolishly not stopping to put on a coat or boots.

Although I did not love Charles, I had grown fond of him. He was a good man in his own way and I wished him no harm.

The wind whipped my nightgown against my legs and the rain lashed out at me until I was soaked through. I walked toward the bank in the direction from which the scream had come. The other cries had stopped altogether. Perhaps it had only been a gull.

I had not gone far, groping through the darkness, when I realized that I could not find my way in this blackest of black nights. I turned around, but could see no light where I thought the house should be. I began to feel my way, cautiously, with every step. I soon found myself struggling through wild bushes that had not yet been cleared away and feared that I was getting close to the bank. Suddenly the very earth seemed to give way beneath my feet. I tumbled down and down, sliding through the darkness, expecting at any moment to splash into the angry waves. My feet landed on hard, cold rock, wet and slippery. I fell back, hitting my head. I remember nothing more until I awoke in the care of a doctor some weeks later.

I had numerous injuries, including some bad head wounds. Dr. Helmcken was convinced that my brain was damaged because I kept talking of hidden tunnels and a ghost that was really alive. I remember none of this.

I suffered for many weeks with pneumonia, and for a time they thought I was sure to die. There was no one familiar to visit me and I felt terribly alone. I asked after my husband and they told me he had disappeared. When I asked after Carlson, the doctor explained that it was he who brought me to the hospital, but no one knew what became of him after that.

During my long period of inactivity, I decided that the tunnel had been used to frighten us away. For what dark purpose, I could not imagine.

Gradually I recovered my health, but Dr. Helmcken consulted with his father-in-law, James Douglas, who is an important man, being governor of the two colonies: Vancouver Island and British Columbia. Those two men decided that I should be sent home. It seems they have no place in the colony for insane people, so they ship them back to England, where, I should imagine, they fit in quite admirably.

The night before my ship was to sail someone came into my room and covered my mouth so I could not scream. When I saw that it was Carlson, I was not frightened. He brought me back to the safety of this cave. Now I can never return to England.

My only regret is that I cannot let my sister know I am alive and happy. Mary sent me a letter that was brought to me in hospital. If I had not foolishly tucked it in with other papers that were delivered to me from the house, I would have it still. However, the next thing I knew, Dr. Helmcken whisked everything away, saying I should not disturb myself with difficult, worldly matters. Women have such tiny wee brains, you see, that "worldly matters" are simply too much for us to handle.

I expect the good doctor blames himself for my disappearance. I understand his theory is that my fragile mind finally snapped and I threw myself off a cliff because I missed dear Charles so!

No one must know where I am or they would ship me off to England and likely arrest Frank for kidnapping. So, for now, we shall continue to hide out here. But things will change — we are making plans to better ourselves.

At last I have my chance to lead a life which is not dull and ordinary!

The next several pages were taken up with Elizabeth's account of how and why Frank Carlson came to live beneath her house.

Early in 1857 a young man named Francisco Carlos left his home in Spain to join the crew of a sailing ship. It was not until the crew raided another ship at sea that Francisco realized he had linked up with pirates.

Six months later they sailed into the Pacific Northwest. The pirates began attacking isolated Native villages.

They stole whatever they could find of value, from animal pelts to dried salmon. Of course, the Spanish ship had superior gun power, and in the skirmishes Native people were sometimes killed.

Finally, on a stormy night in late November, the ship and crew paid for their sins. Just before dark the Spanish ship, heavily laden and low in the water, struck an uncharted rock and began to break up. Francisco, along with most of the crew, made his way to shore, where an angry group waited for them. A fight followed. Of the crew, only Francisco and two others survived. They fled to the cover of trees, where they watched the Natives bury the dead.

When most of the Natives had gone down to the beach, the two pirates rushed out to attack two old men who had been left behind. Francisco hung back — he had never killed a human being and never wanted to. The elders were seasoned warriors and fought hard, killing one of the Spaniards and wounding the other before they too died. In an effort to hide the fact that there were survivors, Francisco hauled the three bodies out of sight and later buried them.

Francisco and his wounded companion hid, wet and cold, all that night and the next day. On the following day, Francisco crept out of the bushes to comb the beach for shellfish. He scoured the bank above the inlet, hoping to find gulls' eggs, but happened instead to spot a small hole in the clay, almost hidden by the hanging roots of a giant fir tree at the top of the bank. He dug with his hands to enlarge the hole until it was big enough to scramble inside. To his amazement, he found it opened into a tunnel that led to a large, dry cave.

The young man helped his companion into the shelter. After enlarging the entrance, Francisco brought a big, round rock from the beach to help camouflage it.

While the other man, Juan, was recovering from his wounds, Francisco began sneaking into houses on the outskirts of nearby Fort Victoria. He helped himself to supplies such as food and lanterns and dishes. At night he would sneak onto one of the farms outside the fort and take vegetables and fruit; he even got bold enough to steal chickens and a live piglet. Francisco became so good at stealing, in fact, that he managed to take warm blankets, clothes, and other much-needed supplies from the Hudson's Bay store right inside the palisades at Fort Victoria.

Soon he began to hang around Esquimalt Harbor, listening and watching. Francisco had studied English at school in Spain and so quickly picked up the language. He practiced repeating words over and over again so he would not have a Spanish accent.

Juan eventually recovered, and they made the cave more comfortable with furniture they built from driftwood, using tools and supplies Francisco obtained. They worked hard to enlarge the inside of their tunnel by chopping back the fir tree's roots, and then they shored up the walls and ceiling with timbers salvaged from the ship's hull. As a precaution, they began work on an escape tunnel. The digging took over seven months, but the completed tunnel led away from the cave on a gradual uphill slope and ended in a vertical shaft hidden in bushes on the hillside.

By the spring of 1858 they were quite comfortable in their home but beginning to get bored. Fort Victoria was still very small and consisted mainly of Hudson's Bay Company employees and their families. Everyone knew each other, which made it impossible for Juan and Francisco to mingle with them. And people were on the lookout, knowing there were thieves in the area, even though most of them blamed the crimes on the Natives who were camped around the fort.

Then, quite suddenly, in April of 1858, everything changed. A ship arrived from San Francisco carrying so many men that the population of Victoria doubled the minute they stepped ashore. The gold mines of California had lost their luster and the men had moved on, following news of rich gold strikes on the Fraser River. From all over the world, men began to converge on Victoria. Most of them purchased supplies and set off for the mainland in search of gold, but some stayed to set up businesses and profit from selling supplies to the gold seekers.

With so many strangers in town, the two Spaniards could wander about freely and help themselves to whatever they needed from the new Victoria stores. They made the cave even more comfortable with rugs and blankets and even a small cookstove. The cave was far enough from town that if they were careful to burn wood only at night and on wet, stormy days, the smoke filtering out through the escape tunnel was not noticed. In fact, the cave was so warm and dry that the men clustered in their cold, damp tents closer to town would have envied them, had they known.

As winter set in, men began to trickle back from the Fraser. Some could not resist bragging about their new-found riches. They spent their money freely in the many saloons Victoria provided. As they made their drunken way home through the dark streets, many met up with two men who relieved them of whatever gold dust remained in their pockets.

It was never enough for Juan, who wanted to return to Spain and live in comfort. And so he convinced Francisco to help him rob the new bank. In spite of their careful planning, however, things went terribly wrong, and Juan was killed in the attempted robbery of MacDonald's Bank.

After that Francisco was on his own. In the spring of 1859, he set out to explore the vast new land. He tried his hand at gold mining on the Fraser, but soon discovered that prospecting was too much work for his liking. He got a job in a coal mine at Fort Rupert, but found the work too hard and the pay too small. He traveled south to Washington Territory, where he found work as a farm hand. But Francisco didn't much like working for a living. It was so much easier to steal what he wanted from the people who had earned it. Whenever he needed to hide out, he always returned to the cave.

He was living there in the fall of 1862 and looking forward to meeting up with men returning from the new gold finds in the Cariboo. His dream was to have enough money by spring to buy his own ship, hire a crew and waylay ships carrying gold to San Francisco. But his plans were upset when work started on the land directly above his home. At first he tried to scare the workmen off by arranging minor accidents. But suddenly the fir tree above his tunnel entrance crashed to the ground, widening the opening and leaving it exposed. Francisco hurried to camouflage it with bushes and rocks. After that he decided to take a job helping with the construction and, so as not to arouse suspicion, he rented a room in a boarding house in town. At that time he changed his name to Frank Carlson.

Working on the house, and returning often at night, gave him the opportunity to add features that were important to him, such as a trapdoor in the kitchen floor, providing an entrance to the cave below.

A year later, when the occupants moved into the house, Frank had another idea. He stole some appropriate clothes from a Victoria store and managed to get a job as the butler. He was a good-looking young man, and his manners were impeccable. His English was perfect. No one suspected that he was behind the strange happenings during construction.

Frank Carlson did not mean to fall in love with Elizabeth Matthews, whom he secretly called Eliza, but they had become good friends, and he knew how perfect she was for him. When he heard the cries that night, he knew they were not human and would have told Sir Charles to stay indoors, if only he had asked. Frank didn't know anything was wrong until early the next morning when he set out to scour the beach, expecting to find another young sheep that had wandered too far from a nearby farm. Instead, he found Elizabeth on the beach, shivering with cold and asking after Charles. He brought her back to the cave but soon realized she needed more help than he could give her, so he took her to Dr. Helmcken. Elizabeth had suffered a concussion and remembered none of this. Although Carlson returned to lead a search party, no sign of Charles was ever found.

While Elizabeth was recovering, Frank began to hang around the hospital. At last he learned that she was well but, to his dismay, was to be sent back to England. That very night Frank sneaked into her room and spirited her away. As it turned out, Elizabeth was quite happy to see him; she had no intention of returning to England.

That summer, the couple booked passage on a ship to San Francisco, traveling as a lady and gentleman. There they married, then returned to Victoria and the cave. Now, under the name Eliza Carlson, she started a new section in her diary.

As Katie read through it, she quickly noticed how Eliza became a completely different person than Elizabeth. Eliza was much less formal and seemed far happier than Elizabeth. No longer bored, she found little time to keep her diary. The writing was hurried and difficult to read. Near the end of the book, Katie found this note:

September 23, 1864

We did it! MacDonald's Bank is now poorer by $30,000! No one knows who did it, but the police suspect it was an inside job!

We are safe here in the cave, as no one else knows about it. Thank goodness we've never had to use that horrid escape tunnel!

Now we have money to build a real home and live in comfort. We'll buy a farm near Sooke, where no one knows me. I can hardly wait. We'll have lots of horses and people will admire us.

We'll also buy a schooner to use for exporting our goods — farm produce and other pieces that turn up now and then. Victoria is growing rapidly and many of its new citizens have expensive tastes.

More wonderful news! We're going to have a child before next summer. I am convinced it will be a son. One day he will become a respected member of the community, perhaps a bank manager or a lawyer. In his spare time, he will help with the family business.

This life is so exciting!

There was only one more entry, dated November 28, 1864:

We're going away to try out our new boat and meet with some Americans who are interested in purchasing the goods we expect to have available. I can hardly wait! Sailing always gives me such a thrill, and I'm becoming a very good sailor.

I plan to bury my diary amongst the rocks in the

tunnel for safekeeping until we return. If I remember to dig it out I'll write in it again, perhaps, but I am losing interest. There is so much to do!

Katie closed the small, leather-bound book and switched off her light.

... twelve ...

Anchors Aweigh

Next morning Sheila phoned. "Want to come to the beach with us?"

"I thought it was just you and your mom."

"Yeah. Well, she's bringing a friend."

"Sure. Okay. Should I bring some food?"

"No, we've got tons. See you in half an hour."

When a car horn honked outside, Katie ran out the door with her bag over her shoulder. She skipped down the front stairs, ran along the sidewalk and then stopped so suddenly she teetered forward and almost fell.

Not Sheila's mom's old blue car, but a sleek, silver sports car crouched in the driveway, its engine purring. Chief Carlson's teeth gleamed in the front window. Behind him, Sheila's face was small and pleading.

Katie glared at her friend as she squeezed into the tiny back seat and settled with her knees around her ears. But it was not until they arrived at Patricia Bay and struggled out of the car that she grabbed Sheila's arm. "Why didn't you tell me who the friend was?"

Sheila stared at the ground. "I was afraid you wouldn't come."

"Then you'd be wrong. This is a perfect opportunity to check Carlson out." Quickly she told Sheila what she had discovered in the diary.

"Come on, I'll build you a raft!" Chief Carlson called to them from the beach below. When they clambered down he was standing beside a big log. Tucked under one arm were several short, flat pieces of driftwood; he held a hammer in one hand and a can of nails in the other.

The girls helped roll the log into the water. They found a second log and floated it up beside the first. Warm salt water lapped about their knees as they laid the pieces of wood across the logs and held them steady. Carlson nailed the first one in place. "My father always built us rafts when we went to the beach," he explained.

"Was he a policeman too?" The question shot out of her mouth before Katie quite realized it was there.

Carlson looked up. Several short nails protruded from his mouth, and he had to spit them into his hand to answer. "No, he was a banker."

Katie rolled her eyes toward Sheila, who carefully ignored her.

Water gurgled around his legs as Carlson waded to the next piece of wood. "My ancestors were among the first families to immigrate to Victoria," he told them proudly. "My great-grandfather was born on a farm out near Sooke in 1865."

"Oh, wow!" said Katie, then quickly added, "A farmer."

"No, actually he was a businessman. Into lots of things."

"I'll bet!" Katie said, and her mouth dropped open. She reached up and pushed it shut with her hand. She hoped it would stay that way.

Her words hung in the warm air like a dark cloud. Carlson glared at her over the raft.

"I mean, I'll bet he did a lot for the economy," she added quickly, and Carlson hammered in another nail.

When the raft was ready they found two long, flat chunks of driftwood for paddles, and Carlson handed them a rope. They chose a large, angular rock, loaded it onto the raft and paddled out into the bay, where they wrapped the rope around it on all four sides, like a ribbon around a birthday present, and tied a good, stout knot at the top. Katie tied the other end to the raft and Sheila dropped their anchor overboard.

The girls put on their masks, snorkels and swim fins, and dived down to check it out. The rock anchor had settled into a bed of soft sand; the rope was secure around it. There was plenty of extra rope lying on the bottom to allow for a tide change. Satisfied, the two kicked up to the surface.

They dived and jumped off the raft; they swam in the shallow, sun-warmed water, snorkeling, ducking under to retrieve stones from the sandy bottom. Finally they crawled onto the raft for a rest, and Katie found herself thinking about Elizabeth Matthews — alias Eliza Carlson. She felt sorry for Elizabeth, but was not so sure she liked Eliza.

The raft tilted, and water sloshed over the side. Katie sat up, dizzy in the bright sun.

On the edge of the raft sat Chief Carlson, his legs dangling in the water. "Been to any haunted houses lately?" he grinned.

Katie swallowed. Sheila stared.

"If you ask me, young girls should stay away from deserted places such as haunted houses. They just might find themselves in trouble."

Katie's throat tightened. She couldn't move — not her head, not so much as her eyes. Then, as if his earlier words had never been spoken, Chief Carlson flashed his wide, white-toothed smile and said, "The water's beautiful today. Did you see any fish?"

Katie managed to nod.

"A few," said Sheila in a strangled voice.

"In that case, may I borrow your mask? I'd like to take a look." Without waiting for an answer, he pulled Sheila's mask over his face and slid into the emerald green water.

"Are you going to tell your mom?" Katie whispered.

Sheila shook her head. "She'd say I was imagining things."

"But he threatened us!"

"All he said was that we might get into trouble if we

kept hanging around deserted houses. Mom would probably agree with him."

"He's smart."

Sheila nodded. "And sneaky."

Something splashed behind them. A flash of sun glinted off the glass diving mask, just above the surface. Carlson pulled off the mask and placed it on the raft. "Take care." He winked, grinned and set off toward shore with strong, sure strokes.

A chill shot down Katie's spine. "I don't trust him," she said. She lay on her stomach, rested her chin on her folded arms and tried to think. Was Carlson really up to no good or was she simply reading something sinister into everything he did? Was he being friendly with Sheila's mother just so he could keep an eye on them? Or, what if he only hung around the old house because he knew his great-great-grandmother once lived there? Maybe he felt it somehow belonged to him.

The white shapes she had seen that first day returned to haunt her now. Was it just a coincidence that they resembled the missing sculptures? Had one of them really moved toward her? She thought so. It could have been someone trying to scare her away. Which brought her right back to the beginning again. Something funny was going on, and Chief Carlson knew more than he was admitting.

A cool breeze made her shiver. Waves gurgled against the raft. Katie sat up. Something had changed. Her first thought was that the tide had gone in a long way, but

that was odd, because it was supposed to be going out. Then she realized the raft was not in the same spot. It had drifted out of the bay and was moving quickly now, caught in the outgoing current. It was being carried toward Satellite Channel, where a strong wind was blowing and waves were building.

On the beach, Sheila's mom, a tiny figure in a green bathing suit, waved her arms frantically. She ran into the water and cupped her hands to her mouth, calling to the girls, but Katie could not hear her over the rising wind. She waved back. It was all she could do. At least Sheila's mother would know they were aware of their danger. Katie looked around for the paddles. They were gone!

Then she spotted one, rising to the top of a wave some distance away.

Sheila was lying on her back, one arm flung over her eyes, breathing evenly. Katie grabbed her shoulder. "Sheila! Sheila, wake up!"

Sheila opened her eyes. "Brrr," she said, and sat bolt upright as a wave broke over the raft. "What's going on?"

"We've drifted out of the bay." Katie looked toward the channel. The wind was stirring up waves and whipping the tops off foaming whitecaps. Dark clouds rolled high overhead. "The paddles washed overboard and a storm is coming up."

"Let's swim for it."

"No. We'd never make it. We've got to stay on the raft."

Sheila nodded. They both knew Katie was right. Even

if the tide were not running so fast, the water out here was too cold to survive in for long. The wind, gathering force as it funneled through Sansum Narrows, hit them full on, chilling them to the bone. The raft creaked and groaned with the action of every wave. Cold water sprayed over their heads.

A nail in one of the pieces of driftwood began to work its way loose. With each successive wave, more of the nail showed. The piece of wood worked itself free and the waves set to work on the next one. The raft, made out of driftwood and intended for calm water, was no match for a stormy sea.

"The raft is breaking up!" Katie yelled.

"I know!"

"What are we going to do?"

"I don't know."

They huddled close together, trying to get warm.

"Mom must have called the coast guard by now."

"Yeah, but they could take an hour to get here."

The raft was twisting itself apart. When one log rose on a wave, the other sank.

"We'll never last that long," said Sheila, watching Katie pull in the anchor rope. They stared at the end that had been tied around the rock. It had not been cut, it had simply come undone.

"Do you think he did it?" Sheila asked.

Katie shrugged. There was no way of proving it either way. "I'm so cold I could scream!" She hugged her knees against her chest.

"Listen," said Sheila, "when the raft breaks up we've both got to hang onto one of the logs. Try to climb up on it."

Katie nodded and clenched her teeth to keep them still.

"Look!" Sheila pointed into the distance. Katie caught a glimpse of white as something slid down a wave and disappeared.

"What?"

"A boat, over there!"

Katie's eyes watered. "It's only a seagull."

"No, there it is again. It's the top of a little boat. I'm sure!"

Katie rubbed her eyes. "Seagull." She was so cold.

Sheila pushed herself unsteadily to her feet and waved her arms above her head. As she did, the raft gave a final, violent lurch and broke apart. Sheila tumbled headfirst into the water.

"Sheila!" Katie screamed. She tried to hold onto a log, but it rolled over and dumped her underwater. The cold shocked her, surrounded her; foul-tasting water filled her mouth and nostrils. She kicked up to the surface. Choking, frantic, she looked for Sheila but saw only a gray wave rolling toward her. "Sheila!" she cried, and swallowed more seawater as the wave broke over her head. She choked and struggled to remain afloat.

As she tired, her head sank below the surface. She must have breathed in, because more of the bitter-tasting salt water caught in her throat, gurgled into her lungs.

Katie lifted her face, gasping for air.

Something grabbed at her from above. She pushed it away. Then something rose up beneath her. It pushed her up out of the water, and then she was pulled roughly from above. She tried to free herself but could not. She slumped down on a cold, hard surface, made an attempt to protest, then lay still.

... thirteen ...

The Disappearance

Darkness enfolded her. So peaceful. So welcoming. Katie drifted into it. She saw her family and called out to them, "Mom! Dad!" But they couldn't hear. "Michael!" she called, but he wouldn't look.

Rusty joined them, but he ignored her too. They all looked so happy ...

They were glad to be rid of her, that was it, especially Rusty and Michael. She should have been nicer to them. "Hey, Mikey!" she called, "you're not such a bad little brother, you know." But he turned and walked away. "And Rusty — I mean, Russ — I'm sorry!" But he paid no attention.

Hands clutched her shoulders. She tried to pull away but they held on stubbornly. A voice began repeating the same words, over and over, senseless, meaningless words. Gradually, she began to understand: "Katie, open your eyes, we love you! Katie, open your eyes, we love you."

As if she were swimming up to the surface, into the sunlight, Katie pushed the darkness away. She forced her eyes open. Three faceless images floated above her, with a light behind them so fiercely bright she could not see. Her eyes fluttered shut.

A big hand, warm and familiar, squeezed hers. "We're here," said her dad. "You're safe in a hospital bed. Katie, please don't go away again."

She opened her eyes, just a crack. The dark, floating images formed into faces, the worried faces of her family. Gently her mom brushed back the curls from Katie's forehead. "Katie," was all she said.

"Can I hug her now?" asked Michael.

Normally Katie would have made a face and pulled away from her little brother. But not then, not even if she could. She smiled — or, at least, thought she smiled. She couldn't be sure because her face muscles didn't seem to be working properly.

"Not just yet," her mom told him. And then, "How do you feel, Katie?"

She tried to say, "Tired," but discovered her voice wasn't working either. Her eyes closed, her eyelids were so heavy.

"Sleep now. We'll be here when you wake up."

She slipped away. Almost. But something was wrong — something she needed to know. "Shla ..." she managed.

Her mother understood. "Sheila's fine. She's in the next room."

Katie drifted into a deep, untroubled sleep.

Much later she discovered she had slept for a whole night and most of the next day. It was early evening. Michael had gone to their grandparents' house, but her parents were still here, still sitting by her bed. They looked so much older than they had a few days ago and so horribly pale, with dark circles under their eyes, that Katie scarcely recognized them. They rose wearily to their feet.

"Are we going home now?" She sat up in bed.

"The doctor wants you to stay in another night," her mom explained. "We're going home to get some sleep, but we'll be back in the morning"

. . . . . .

The following morning Katie woke up very early. The hospital was quiet and dark — a perfect time for thinking. She thought about Chief Carlson and the diary and the accident with the raft. If it *was* an accident. She thought about all the things she knew, and all she suspected, and decided it was time to tell her parents. She could be wrong, of course, but seeing Sheila disappear into that cold water had frightened her, and she knew this was no time for secrets.

But when her parents and Michael finally arrived, they were not alone. Katie took one look and wanted to dive under the covers.

"Katie!" Chief Carlson said, striding into the room, his dazzling smile firmly in place. "I hear you're going home today. That's fantastic! How do you feel?"

"Uh …" She studied her hands, her fingers twisted into the white sheet. "Okay."

"Katie," her mom said, "aren't you going to thank Chief Carlson for saving your life?"

What? Her head jerked up and her mouth fell open. They thought Carlson *saved* her life? He winked, and she turned to look out the tiny, square window.

"Well, Katie," he said, "I just stopped by to say hello. I'm driving Sheila and her mother home, so I'd better go now. Stay out of trouble." He lightly squeezed her foot through the hospital blankets. She jerked her leg away and refused to look at him.

"Katie Reid," her mother said after he had gone, "how can you be so rude? That wonderful man saved your life!"

Katie bit her lip. Suddenly Carlson was a hero! Who would believe her now if she told them he had untied the rope?

In the car on the way home, her parents told her about Chief Carlson, how he had rushed to borrow a small boat from an old fisherman and, with Sheila's mother, raced out into the storm to rescue the girls. Hed risked his life by diving into the rough water and handing each of the girls up to Ms. Walton.

"While Elaine drove the boat back to shore," Katie's mother said, her voice all scratchy as if she had a cold, "Chief Carlson gave you mouth-to-mouth resuscitation."

"Yuck!" Katie wiped her sleeve across her mouth. Suddenly she felt sick.

• • • • • •

After two days at home, Katie was getting bored, so she was glad when Rusty phoned after lunch.

"Did you see the paper today?"

"No."

"Did you hear what happened?"

"No."

"Two policemen disappeared last night!"

"Oh!"

"Can you guess who they are?"

"No."

"You'll never believe it! Spike Davis and Archie McFee! And — this is spooky — their car was parked back at the station, even though no one saw them come in from their shift!"

"Oh!"

"And, guess what else? The art gallery was broken into and robbed last night. Millions of dollars' worth of art was stolen."

"Oh!"

"So, you were wrong! I was right — it was those two cops who did it, and they've taken off with all the loot! Never to be seen again!"

Katie gasped but could not answer. She felt sick inside. How could she be so wrong?

"One more thing, but not so exciting. I found out that the old house is going to be torn down next week. The owners in England sold it to a developer and he's going to build a subdivision there."

"Oh, no!"

Rusty paused for a moment. "Can't you say anything but 'oh' and 'no'?"

"No. Oh! Of course I can. Listen, Rusty, we've got to meet at the fort. I'll phone Sheila. Be there in an hour."

As Katie replaced the receiver after talking to Sheila, she heard a scuffling noise in the hall. It was followed by light footsteps scurrying away. "Michael, I know you were listening!" she yelled, and hurried out of the kitchen. But Michael was up in his bedroom, singing, "Row, row, row your boat …"

• • • • • •

"Okay," said Rusty when they were settled in the fort. "We know who did it, now we just need to figure out where they are."

"You've got it backward," Katie told him. "We know *where* they are, we just can't agree on *who* they are. All that art stuff will be at the house, waiting until they can smuggle it away, which will have to be soon."

Rusty shook his head. "If those cops didn't do it, then where are they?"

"I bet they saw something they shouldn't have and got kidnapped. I just know Carlson is behind this — it's a family tradition."

Rusty gave her a strange look, and Katie realized he knew nothing of the diary, of finding the tunnel, or even

the ghostly white shapes, so she quickly explained everything to him, including their suspicion that Carlson
had untied the anchor rope.

Rusty frowned. "It doesn't make any sense. Why would
he untie the rope and then race out and rescue you?"

"Two reasons: he wanted to scare us *and* he wanted
to look like a hero to our parents — so they wouldn't
listen to us."

"It didn't work," said Sheila so softly no one heard.

"Maybe the two cops are in on it with Carlson."

"Maybe," Katie agreed. "Either way, we have to go
back to the house and look in that front window." She
jumped to her feet. "Let's go!"

As they filed out of the fort, the nearby bushes rustled.

"Must be a raccoon," said Katie.

• • • • • •

They hid their bikes in thick bushes near the top of the
hill and started down Rotten Road. At the final bend,
they all stopped at once. "If anyone's down there, they'll
see us as soon as we round this bend," Rusty whispered.

"That's why we're going through the bushes," said
Katie, diving into the thick salal beside the road.

It was tough going, fighting their way through salal
that grew as high as their heads. The bushes were beaded
with moisture from a soft drizzle that had been falling
since early morning, and Katie was glad of the jacket her
mother had forced her to wear. She walked slowly, for

once not caring that the others were ahead of her. She was worried now as she had not been before. This was no longer a game, and they all needed to be very careful. If either Rusty or Sheila got hurt, it would be her fault because she got them into this in the first place. Lost in her thoughts, she didn't pay much attention to where she was going. Near the bottom of the hill she almost tripped over Sheila. Her friend was bent over, carefully parting the bushes in front of her.

"Where's Rusty?"

"He vanished! Right in front of my eyes!" Sheila's voice came out more high pitched than usual.

"What?"

"He pushed in front of me and suddenly, poof!" Sheila snapped her fingers. "He was gone!"

Then they heard it. A hollow, echoing cry that seemed to begin deep beneath the earth and rise up through the bushes in front of them. All the tiny hairs on the back of Katie's neck stood on end. She glanced at Sheila, whose freckles stood out like brown paint spattered on ghostly white paper.

"Heeelp meeee!"

Katie dropped to her knees and crawled forward, feeling her way cautiously, one hand at a time. One minute there was solid ground beneath her hand, the next there was nothing. She pushed the bushes aside.

Little bits of old, rotten wood lay scattered around a deep, dark hole in the ground, like a large rabbit's burrow, just big enough for a person to fall through. A damp, musty smell rose up from it, along with Rusty's voice, complaining bitterly. "It's slimy down here! Ahh — something's tickling my legs! I think it's worms! Get me out!"

Katie lay on the ground and leaned as far as she could into the hole. She stretched her arms down but could not reach her cousin. "Hey!" she yelled. "Lift up your hands!"

"I *am* lifting up my hands. What do you think? I'm trying to climb out, but there's nothing to hold onto but these little sharp sticks. I'm stuck!"

"Are you hurt?"

"No. But I hate this! It's all mucky down here! And these worms are getting hungry!" He paused and his voice went very small. "Can you get me out?"

"Of course we can." Sheila knelt beside Katie, leaning toward the hole in the ground. "If you could just try to relax, we'll tell you what we're going to do." She leaned closer to Katie and whispered, "What are we going to do?"

"Relax? That's easy for you to say! You're not about to be devoured by giant boy-eating worms!" yelled Rusty.

Katie tried to think. She slipped off her knapsack and opened it, looking for her flashlight. They could haul him up — if only they had a rope. "Hey," she said, taking off her jacket, "I have an idea."

While Sheila had tied their two jackets together by the sleeves and double-checked the knots, Katie shone her flashlight down the hole. A white face looked up at her, with two dark holes where the eyes should be. "Ahhh!" she screamed, and dropped the light.

Rusty's scream blended with hers. Then the flash-light hit him on the head and he yelled, "Ow!" The light went out.

"What?" asked Sheila.

"A skeleton!" Katie whispered. "Down there! It's not worms tickling him, it's bones!"

"Ohhh! Get me out of here!"

They lowered the jackets. "Tell us when you can reach my sleeve," Katie called.

"Got it." Rusty was almost two jacket lengths below ground level. "Hurry! I'm scared!"

"Can you tie the bottom sleeve around your waist?" asked Sheila.

"No! It's not long enough! Oh, wait!"

They listened to scuffling, grunting sounds. "Okay, my knapsack's off. I'm working on my jacket."

"Good thinking. We'll lower our jackets a little more. The thing is, they might rip if you don't help us. So tie yours around your middle and then tie my sleeve tight at the front. That way you can use your arms and legs for climbing."

"Hold my legs," Katie said to Sheila. Gripping a jacket sleeve, she wriggled forward into the hole. She felt a tug on the jacket.

"Rusty?"

"Okay. I did it. It's tied. Now get me out of here!"

Katie pulled and wriggled backward, with Sheila yanking on her legs. Rusty helped from below, and they gradually worked him toward the surface. When his head and shoulders finally appeared above ground, his face was dirty and there were pieces of something wet and dark and slimy clinging to his hair.

Sheila and Katie grabbed his arms and pulled him to safety. "You okay?"

"I guess so. Better than that other guy!"

"Good," Katie told him, "because we have work to do."

"Not before I go down to the beach and wash," said Rusty.

"Good idea," Katie told him. "You stink!"

· · · · · ·

While they were watching Rusty clean up, Katie had a sudden thought. "Hey! You know what?" she called. "I bet you found the escape tunnel. And … could be you found Charles Matthews too!"

Rusty didn't answer; he just splashed more water over his head.

They walked along the beach, close to the bank where they were hidden from the house. Near the dock and entrance to the cave, they stopped and sat in a row, leaning against the bank.

"What now?" Sheila whispered.

"We've got to go up there and look in the windows," Katie explained. "I bet we'll see the stolen art."

"I say we call the police," Rusty suggested. "Didn't you notice? Those bushes I told you about are piled up again. I bet someone's in the house right this minute."

"Yeah, but what would we say?" Katie held her hand to her ear, as if clutching a telephone receiver. "Hello, Police …? Yes, my friends and I think the chief of police, with help from the director, robbed the art gallery last night. Oh, and two police officers too … Yes … And right now they're holed up in a haunted house."

"Mom might believe us," Sheila said quietly.

"Why should she?" Rusty asked. "I thought she liked him."

Sheila shrugged. "She's been asking questions, like why was he hanging around the raft. I told her what he said."

"Well, so — what did she say?" Katie demanded.

Sheila shrugged again. "Not much."

"I say we go phone her now." Rusty jumped up. "Is she at work?"

Sheila nodded and stood up too.

"Shh," said Katie. "Listen!"

They all heard it then, a swish of tires accompanied by a high-pitched, childish voice singing, "Row, row, row your boat …"

"Oh, no!" Katie scrambled up to peek over the bank. And there was Michael, riding his bike toward the house, singing to himself in his off-key voice. He was too far away for Katie to call him without being heard from the house. He stopped at the gate, hesitated, then turned and walked toward the bank on the far side of the peninsula. He laid down his bike and stood very still, looking out over the strait.

Suddenly it made sense. The scuffling outside the kitchen, the bushes rustling near the fort … Of course. Michael had been eavesdropping and had followed them. Katie needed to get him out of sight before someone looked out and saw him. She started to climb up the bank, but the creak of a rusty door hinge made her shrink out of sight.

The door opened. A man filled the doorway, a man so tall he needed to duck to get through the door. His arm muscles bulged below the short sleeves of his T-shirt. His black, wavy hair fell over his forehead. This giant of a man was looking directly at Michael.

Behind him, the short, stout figure of Mr. Anderson waddled out.

"I was right!" Katie whispered.

Anderson pointed toward Michael and said something to the big man.

"Hey, kid!" the man yelled. "Come here a minute."

Michael's head jerked around. He started to back away.

Anderson stepped in front of the big man. "Don't be afraid, son," he said in a gentle voice. "We just want to talk to you."

Michael kept backing away.

When the big man rushed past Anderson and down the stairs, Katie started up the bank. Michael turned and ran.

Two sets of hands pulled Katie back down, out of

... fourteen ...

To the Rescue

Katie eased herself up and peeked over the top of the bank. The house loomed above her, uglier than ever, its windows a hundred tiny eyes staring back, dark and filled with menace. Katie shuddered.

"We need a plan," said Sheila.

"Okay," Rusty suggested, "how about this? One of us should go for help and two of you should stay here and keep an eye on things just in case something happens. You know, like —"

"I'm going in and there's no way you can stop me." Katie scrambled up the bank. Just as she reached the top, there was a loud creak and the front door opened. She slipped back down, until only her eyes were above the bank, hidden by long grass. Rusty scrambled up beside her, clutching Katie's notebook.

They watched the plump figure of Anderson walk purposefully down the stairs. He hurried toward the pile of bushes, stopped and looked all around, then reached up and started pulling branches away. In a few minutes he had uncovered a black pickup truck. He climbed inside, the engine roared into life, and the truck crept forward and stopped in front of the house.

"They're going to take Michael somewhere. How will we ever find him again? I've got to stop them now!"

"If they were going to take him in the truck, they wouldn't have put him in the house," Sheila pointed out. "You've just got to be patient."

But Katie was on the edge of panic. "That's *my* little brother in there and I'm not going to let him get kidnapped just because you're so scared!"

The front door slammed and the big man ran down the stairs alone. He squeezed into the waiting truck. Katie and Rusty ducked out of sight as the truck passed by. Rusty scribbled in the notebook.

"Now we go inside," said Katie.

Rusty snapped the book shut. "I got the license number and a description of the truck. Maybe I should go find a phone," he suggested.

Katie nodded and he was off, running down the beach with her notebook tucked under one arm. She glanced at her open knapsack and frowned, wondering why he had taken her book. Rusty began to struggle up the bank and Katie watched him go, hoping they would meet again soon, both of them alive and well. She swallowed hard and turned to Sheila. Her friend's face was dead white behind that mass of brown freckles. Katie waited for her to object, but Sheila only sucked in her breath, turned her eyes toward the house and nodded.

They climbed up the bank together, ran across the short stretch of ground, and up the front stairs. Sheila reached for the door latch. It wouldn't move. She pushed on the door and wriggled the latch, but it was no use. The door was firmly locked. She glanced over her shoulder.

"The tunnel. Come on!" Katie darted back down the stairs.

They found the same levers they had used before and pried open the door. They crept inside and pulled the door closed after them. Slowly, feeling their way, they moved along the tunnel, across the cave and to the bottom of the stairs. Sheila tiptoed up with Katie close behind. She pushed on the trapdoor. It refused to move.

Katie squeezed beside her to help, and they managed to open the heavy door enough for Katie to work her head and shoulders through. She glanced quickly around at a huge, old-fashioned kitchen. A gigantic wood-burning stove, grimy and draped with cobwebs, lurked in the far corner. The one small window was so dirty that very little light penetrated to lessen the gloom. The air was heavy with a musty odor that made breathing unpleasant. She squeezed through and held the trapdoor open for Sheila.

Together they lowered the heavy door into its square hole and stepped back in amazement. The door settled so perfectly into the lines and grooves of the old wooden floor that it was almost completely camouflaged. One side of it ended at the threshold to the pantry. Because the wood was slightly higher than the flat pantry floor, a person could easily slip a wedge beneath the trapdoor to open it. People might walk over the door day after day for years and never guess it was there.

"Let's go upstairs," Katie whispered, and led the way to the front hall.

They tiptoed past a new collection of white shapes and crept up the winding staircase, sticking so close together that Katie, for once in the lead, could feel Sheila's breath on the back of her neck. At the top they stopped to peer down a wide, gloomy hallway with a high, curved ceiling. There were several doors on each side of the hall, every one of them shut tight. Above each door a stained-glass window let in an eerie light from the room beyond.

The house must have been quite grand when it was new, and Katie could not help but wonder how Elizabeth had felt when she first stood at the top of these stairs and gazed down the wide hall, sparkling clean and glowing in warm lamplight. Each door must have hidden a wonderful new room to be discovered. Now, any one of them could be hiding a frightened little boy. Each door had to be opened and every room searched.

Katie turned the knob of the first door, and it groaned open. A cloud of dust floated into her face. Light streamed through a dirty window and illuminated a huge, barren room that once must have been beautiful but was now decorated with thick cobwebs drooping from the ceiling and making lacy patterns over the window. The girls searched each room. Some were a little bigger and some a little smaller, but every one was empty except for dust, spiders, and their webs. The grandest room, at the end of the hall, with a wide window overlooking the sea, Katie imagined to have been Elizabeth's bedroom. She could almost see Elizabeth slip out of bed while the wind raged outside her window. In her nightgown she must have run through this very door, down the stairs and out into the night.

A hand on her arm made her jump. "Let's go," whispered Sheila.

At the other end of the hall they discovered a second set of stairs. This one was dark and very narrow, at the back of the house, behind the kitchen.

"This must have been for the servants," Katie whispered as they tiptoed gingerly up the steep, dark stairway. At the top they found a hallway very different from the one below. This one was narrow and almost completely dark, with a low ceiling. The air was unbearably hot and stuffy even on this overcast day. The girls groped their way along the wall in almost total darkness until they came to the first door. Katie found the doorknob and pushed. The door stuck. She pushed harder. It burst open.

The room was tiny, scarcely big enough for a narrow bed and dressing table. The window was so small and so close to the floor that whoever slept there would need to get down on hands and knees just to see out. Making the room seem even smaller was its low ceiling, which sloped sharply down to the window. A rough post stood in the room's exact center and supported a heavy beam.

The two girls examined room after room, each one very much like the first. They left each door open to allow light from the windows into the dark hallway.

There were only two rooms left. Katie was almost afraid to open the next door, not because of what might be there, but because of what might *not be* there. Her hand trembled as she reached for the doorknob. She touched it and pulled away. A quick breath in and out, then she grabbed the doorknob, turned it and pushed open the door. She leapt back in surprise.

"Hey! I know you!" Sheila elbowed her way around Katie toward the two men who sat back to back on the floor with a square post between them. Each of their wrists was tied to one of the other man's wrists, so that their arms encircled the post. Their mouths were tightly gagged.

Sheila knelt and undid one of the gags. "Spike Davis?"

"Right. Aren't you Elaine Walton's girl?"

Sheila undid the other man's gag. "And Archie McFee. The two missing policemen."

"You kids will be missing too if you don't get out of here in a hurry."

"We'll take you with us," Katie said, crouching to untie the ropes. But her fingers told her what her eyes had missed in the half-light. They touched hard, cold metal.

"Oh, no!" she gasped.

"Just wait till they hear about this down at the station," said Spike Davis. "Bound with our own handcuffs!

We'll never live it down!"

"I just hope we *live* to not live it down," added his partner. Then he turned to the girls. "The only way you two can help us is to get out of here and call 911. You can't free us without the key, and the key is in Frank Carlson's pocket."

"Carlson?" Katie gasped.

McFee nodded. "Chief Carlson's son. He caught us here last night. This is no place for kids, and you two better get out before it's too late. "

"But my brother!" Katie cried. "They brought my little brother in here. I can't leave without him."

"That must be what we heard. Someone dragged a bundle into the room across the hall less than an hour ago. Could be your brother."

"Get out of here," McFee ordered brusquely. "Take your brother and run. Good luck!"

Katie was already running. She flung open the door across the hall. There, on the floor, cringing against the rough post, his eyes huge with fright, was Michael.

"Mikey!" Katie shouted, and ran over to untie the ropes that bound her little brother. She could feel him trembling as she undid the gag. His skin was cold and clammy, and his damp brown curls stuck to his forehead.

"Katie—" his voice was barely audible "—I'm scared."

"I know." Katie hugged him closer than she had since Michael was a baby. "We all are. That's why we've got to get out of here fast." She helped him up. "Let's go. Follow Sheila. I'll be right behind you."

Michael sniffed. He hesitated, and his eyes suddenly overflowed with tears. Katie forced herself to remain calm. There was no time to lose. She looked at Sheila, who stood in the doorway shifting impatiently from one foot to the other. Katie nodded at her. Sheila turned away. Her footsteps echoed down the hall. To Katie's relief, Michael ran after her.

Sheila led the way down the narrow stairway to the second floor, where she stopped and looked back. "Let's try the front door."

They raced along the wide hallway and down the open staircase. Sheila reached the front door and peeked out through the stained glass. She leapt back as though it was red hot.

"Someone's coming!" she hissed as she raced back, heading for the kitchen.

Sheila clambered down the steps below the trapdoor and Michael followed. Katie stopped, sensing danger. How had Sheila opened the trapdoor so quickly? Behind her the front door rattled; she had no choice. She was halfway down the steps before she saw Sheila standing at the bottom, with Michael close behind. Why didn't they run for the tunnel?

Joists supporting the floor above blocked her view of the cave. She bent down. Her stomach twisted. On the cave floor, standing beside a beautiful marble sculpture, was Chief Carlson, his thumbs hooked into the pockets of his jeans. A flashlight on the post cast an eerie light, creating long shadows and deep, dark corners.

"So, you've come back," Carlson said, his face tight with anger. "I warned you to mind your own business, but you just won't quit, will you?" He moved toward the stairs, his fists clenched at his sides. "I've always believed children must learn to do as they are told."

With one foot, Katie felt for the step behind her. Slowly she raised herself up. One more step and then another.

"Hold it right there!" bellowed Carlson. Katie spun away and darted up the last two steps. She pulled herself through to the kitchen, scrambled to her feet and raced for the front door.

She turned the doorknob. The door refused to open. Her fingers shook as she fumbled with the lock. Finally a metallic click told her it had released. She pulled the door open. Something closed around her arm. Fingers. Warm and dry and very big.

"NO!" she screamed, and swung around. Her teeth found the flesh of a hairy arm and dug in savagely.

"OW!" the man yelled, but held on even more tightly. Katie spit out the hairy arm and looked up into the face of the huge man who had carried Michael away. His expression surprised her. He didn't look scary or cruel — he didn't even look angry. His dark brown eyes gazed down at her with an odd, almost gentle expression. Could it be sympathy?

She tried to pull away, but he picked her up as if she weighed no more than a rag doll. The door slammed shut. She peeked over the big man's shoulder.

Leaning back against the door and looking up at her

with sad, droopy eyes was Mr. Anderson. "You should never have come back here," he sighed.

The big man nodded. "I tried to scare you off the first time. Kids are supposed to be scared of ghosts."

"Ghosts? Oh, right! You mean some big nerd with a sheet draped over his head?" The grip on her arms tightened. Oops! Maybe she shouldn't have said that.

"Chuck, you'll have to take her down to your father," Anderson said.

"You won't get away with this. The police know all about you."

"You're right," Anderson replied in his soft, sad voice. "Two policemen do know, not to mention the police chief himself. But I don't think any of them will be talking. Do you?"

As Chuck carried her, punching and kicking, past the white, shrouded objects, everything fell into place in her mind. She knew exactly what these men were up to.

"So, Charles," said Carlson as the big man bundled Katie down the stairs. "It's nice to see you do something right for a change." He gestured across the cave. "Tie her up with the others."

Charles? Of course. Chuck was a nickname for Charles. Carlson must have thought he was pretty clever naming his son Charles after Sir Charles Matthews, the first owner of the house.

Under Chief Carlson's watchful eye, Chuck bound Katie's hands and feet with a stout rope. He sat her between Sheila and Michael, who were also bound hand

and foot. And so they sat, three in a row, in front of an out-of-the-way alcove in the wall of the cave. The men continued going up and down the stairs, carrying stolen goods down to the cave.

"You'd better let us go," warned Sheila when Chief Carlson came near and bent to put down a sculpture. "My mother will come looking for us."

"I don't think so. You see, she doesn't know where you are." He straightened up and smiled his wide, dazzling smile. Katie glared at him, sickened by that smile — the perfect mask to hide his true ugliness.

"Well …" Sheila's forehead crinkled. "She'll soon figure it out when I don't come home for supper. I told her about the house — and the raft."

For a fraction of a second Carlson looked startled, and his eyes grew fierce, but he quickly composed his face and smiled in his kindly way, as though he were a favorite uncle. "My dear girl," he spoke gently, "aren't you forgetting something? Your mother is on duty until midnight. And long before midnight we will have vanished forever." He started back up the steps, laughing. "Another mysterious disappearance."

... fifteen ...

Trapped

Katie worked at the rope that bound her. Almost, she thought, she could almost squeeze her left hand out. But not quite. Not yet. The rope was rough, and it rubbed against her wrists until they felt raw and she was sure they must be bleeding. She had to get loose. Just a little more time, that's all she needed. She closed her eyes and concentrated on the rope. She was sure Chuck had not tied it as tightly as he could have, but with his father watching so closely, he had done a good enough job.

When most of the stolen artwork had been carried down to the cave, Carlson walked over. He towered above the children.

"I trust you are all enjoying your visit?" he asked.

So polite, thought Katie, glaring up at his smooth, smiling face. He sounded so polite it made her stomach turn.

A loud thump on the stairs made everyone look. The

huge figure of Chuck Carlson was wrestling a gigantic piece of sculpture down the narrow steps.

"Where did the kids come from?" A voice came from the darkened tunnel as a fourth man moved into the lighted cave. He was tall, wearing a captain's hat and a heavy, navy blue turtleneck. Katie recognized him right away as the third man from the restaurant.

"So, you drive the boat," she said. "It must be almost high tide."

His black eyes stared stonily into hers, then flicked toward Carlson.

"It's those nosy kids I told you about," Carlson told him. "They don't know when to quit."

"We'll have to get rid of them," said the captain in a matter-of-fact-tone.

"I don't think so. We'll just leave them here. Someone's sure to find them before the place is demolished next week, and by then we'll be long gone."

The captain took off his cap and scratched his head. "Sounds dangerous. If someone finds them too soon, they'll ruin all our plans. I'm not about to give up the boat of my dreams for a few nosy little brats. I've worked too hard for it."

"You might be right, Frank," Carlson answered, rubbing his chin thoughtfully. "Elaine Walton will probably have things figured out pretty quickly, knowing what she knows, and it looks as if these kids are too smart for their own good. As soon as the police find them, every police force and the coast guard in both countries will be out looking for us. And then there are those interfering cops upstairs. I ordered them to stay away from here —"

"We've all worked hard," Anderson interrupted. "And taken a lot of risks over the years. But you can't hurt the children. I won't let you."

The captain and the chief looked at each other. They grinned. Then they both turned and laughed down at the sad, plump figure of Anderson. For the first time, Katie noticed the similarity between their two faces, Carlson's and the captain's. The same crinkled eyes when they laughed, the same straight, white teeth and wide, grinning mouths. Carlson had called him Frank. He must be Frank Carlson, the chief's other son. Carlson was so proud of his ancestors, he had named his own son after the first of the Carlson dynasty. Remembering the handcuff key, Katie studied Frank's chest pocket. Something narrow and black protruded from it, like the top of a pen.

"And exactly what do you plan to do about it?" the captain asked Anderson.

Before he could answer, Chuck dropped the heavy sculpture at Chief Carlson's heels. He glared down at the two tall men, making them look small and frail beside his enormous bulk. "He can tell me about it, that's what. We don't hurt kids."

"My brother, the wimp," said Frank, shaking his head and turning away in disgust.

Carlson glared up at his younger son. "I should have known better than to name you Charles," he said. "You're weak. Weak and foolish like Charles Matthews."

Chuck frowned down at his father, his eyes narrowed, and then slowly he smiled. "Want to know what I think? I think taking stupid orders from you is what makes me weak."

Carlson obviously didn't want to get into a family argument. "We'll decide what to do with them later," he said impatiently. "Right now we've got work to do."

Slipping his hand inside his jacket, Carlson pulled out a small gun. "Anderson, you guard the kids," he ordered, holding out the gun. "If any one of them escapes I'm holding you personally responsible."

The plump man reached out with a trembling hand and took the gun. He held it at arm's length, away from his body and pointing toward the floor as though it had a life of its own and could not be trusted.

Chief Carlson eyed the gun as if he were already sorry for handing it to Anderson. "Just keep those kids out of our way," he said, placing a hand on Anderson's shoulder and digging his fingers into the soft flesh until the chubby man winced. "And keep your fat fingers away from that trigger."

· · · · · ·

The men worked quickly, moving back and forth, carrying the valuable pieces of art through the tunnel and out to the waiting boat. Katie watched them carefully. They seldom bothered to glance toward the children — in fact, they seemed to have forgotten all about them.

Anderson too paid them little attention as he watched the others work. Beside her, Michael whimpered quietly.

"Don't worry," she whispered, "I'll have us out of here in no time."

"Really?" Sheila asked.

Katie bit her lip. "Yes," she said, and worked harder than ever at the rope tying her wrists. Almost there. She pulled and twisted, pulled and twisted. It felt as though all the skin was being scraped off her wrists. But she was nearly free. She pulled her right hand up, twisted, and the rope came loose.

A large painting was moving toward the tunnel mouth. Below it a pair of legs, wearing jeans, strode swiftly along; above it the top of a captain's cap was just visible. When it disappeared, there was only one man left in the cave. Katie studied him. Anderson stared wistfully toward the tunnel, tapping the handgun against the side of his leg. Katie leaned close to her brother.

"Shh," she warned. "If I tell you something, do you promise to keep quiet?"

He nodded.

"Good. My hands are free. I'm going to untie Sheila first, then you."

Michael's head swung around, his eyes wide, his mouth open, ready to protest.

"Shh," she said again. "I need you to watch the tunnel. If anyone comes, or Anderson turns this way, give a cough. Okay?"

Michael nodded, and Katie wriggled a little closer to

Sheila. She leaned over to work at the rope. But the knots were tight and difficult to see in the poor light. "This is going to take a few minutes," she whispered. She worked at the knot. It had just begun to loosen when Michael coughed. Katie sat up quickly, her hands behind her back.

Footsteps rattled against loose stones. Anderson shook himself as if just waking from a dream and turned to look at the children with his droopy eyes. Katie sat very still, her hands behind her back.

Chief Carlson strode into the cave, glanced at Anderson and bent to pick up two small paintings. As Carlson's footsteps retreated down the tunnel, Anderson stepped closer to the children. He looked from face to face. Then, seeming satisfied, he turned his back on them. At that moment Katie heard a sound so faint she might have imagined it.

She leaned back, almost lying on the rocks, to look more closely at the alcove behind them. It cut further into the rock than she had at first realized. The rock ceiling sloped down at a steep angle to meet the floor. In the low corner, a dark shadow made it look as if … Wait! A flash of light, quick as lightning, and then that faint sound again.

"Hey!" whispered Sheila. "Are you going to untie me or what?"

Katie sat up and set to work. The knot began to loosen. "We're almost out of here!" she told Sheila a few minutes later. Michael coughed.

The three of them sat perfectly still as Chuck walked into the cave. He stopped and looked at the children.

"Don't even think of doing anything stupid!" His father's voice rang hollowly through the tunnel.

Chuck picked up the huge stone and wire sculpture he had earlier dropped at his father's feet. It was an odd-looking piece that Katie thought would fit better in a junkyard than an art gallery. Chuck struggled toward the tunnel with it. As soon as he had disappeared, Sheila leaned forward to untie her legs. Katie turned and undid her brother's ropes.

"Now what?" whispered Sheila.

Michael coughed. They left the ropes wrapped around their ankles and sat up, hands behind their backs.

Frank Carlson entered the main part of the cave and picked up a delicate figurine. It was one of the few remaining pieces. He wrapped it carefully in paper, placed it in a box and glared in their direction.

Chief Carlson's voice echoed through the tunnel. "Frank, let's get out of here! The tide's turning — we're running out of time!"

Frank ran into the tunnel. "Hey! Give me a little help here? We need to take some hostages with us."

Michael gasped. Katie scooped up her ropes and Michael's, grabbed his hand and jumped up, yanking him roughly to his feet. "Bring your ropes. Follow us," she told Sheila, and ran for the back corner of the alcove, dragging her brother behind her.

"I have to be right. I have to be right. Please let me

be right," she whispered as she ducked under the low ceiling at the back of the alcove.

"What are you doing?" asked Sheila.

"The escape tunnel. I'm sure the entrance is here, and I think —"

"Stop right there!" an angry voice yelled. Footsteps struck against the stone floor behind them.

"Right here!" cried a voice, and a thin, white hand appeared in the rectangular black hole in front of them. Sheila threw herself onto her stomach. She slithered forward, quickly disappearing into the dark under a ledge of rock.

"Your turn!" said Katie, pushing her brother forward.

"No!" he whined. "I can't!"

"Look!" She grabbed him by the shoulders. "It's either that or a boat ride with these guys. You'll never reach the other side."

Michael glanced at the shallow opening, like the mouth of a shark, waiting. He threw himself down and an arm reached out to help him through.

"Stop!" The voice was so close behind her, Katie expected a hand to grab her around the neck. She threw herself forward with her arms flung out in front of her head. Hands grabbed her wrists and started to drag her over the rocky ground. She was under the ledge, squeezing through the opening, with little room to spare. Suddenly a powerful hand grabbed her foot.

"I'm gonna teach you a lesson, kid," Frank growled.

Katie twisted her foot hard, pulled forward and

pointed her toes. Her shoelace must have been loose, because her foot slipped right out of the shoe and she was dragged out of reach.

"Katie," said a familiar voice. "You okay?"

"Hey, Rusty! I thought it was you!"

"I saw them coming before I reached my bike, so I came back to help!"

A terrible noise came from behind them then, an animal-like howl of anger. This was followed by a great deal of grunting and a frantic scrambling and scratching over rock.

"Hey, Frank," Katie said, "betcha can't get us!"

Rusty laid a hand on her arm and pulled. "Let's get out of here!"

"In a minute." She waited. More grunting and the clatter of loose rocks. Then the words she had been waiting for. "Oh, God! I'm stuck! I can't move my arms! Get me out of here!" Frank wailed.

"You got a flashlight?" asked Katie.

Rusty handed it to her. "It was in my knapsack, in the tunnel."

Katie switched it on and moved toward Frank Carlson. His breathing was loud and very quick. He lay flat on his stomach with his arms trapped beneath him, wedged tightly in the opening to the escape tunnel, unable to move. She crouched in front of him. Her hand shook as she reached down toward his chest pocket. Her fingers touched the pen-like object, wrapped around it and pulled.

"Hey!" he yelled, and tried to move. He groaned as he found himself more firmly stuck.

"Thanks, Frank," Katie said. "I don't suppose you'd like to hand me my shoe?"

He growled.

"Guess not. Don't worry —" she held up his cell phone "— we'll call for help as soon as we get out of here."

He growled again as Rusty pulled her away and took the flashlight.

Sheila and Michael were waiting for them. Beyond them the tunnel narrowed again, until it was barely wide enough for one person and not much higher than their waists.

"Come on!" Sheila whispered, and moved deeper into the tunnel. The flashlight's beam played along the rocky floor and walls.

Katie, following Rusty at the end of the line, heard shouting from behind. She stopped to listen. Chuck's voice boomed, "I can't move him! He's stuck tight! We can't get at the kids either!"

Fainter and farther away, Chief Carlson's voice echoed through the tunnel. "We'll get you out, son. Don't worry!"

That's when Katie realized that the Carlsons did not know about the escape tunnel. Strange, after all these years, that she would know about it and not them. But of course, they didn't have the diary, so they must think she and the others were trapped in here.

The tunnel went on forever. Katie tried to quiet the fear in her stomach. She was terrified of being underground, bent double, following the distant scuffling sounds. She almost felt sorry for Frank.

Then suddenly there was light up ahead. Rusty was sitting at the end of the horizontal tunnel, shining his light on Sheila and Michael, who were both standing, squeezed into the vertical shaft Rusty had fallen into earlier. At their feet lay a skull and broken bones.

"Now what do we do?" asked Sheila.

"That's why we brought the ropes," Katie told her, pas-ing them over Rusty's shoulder. "Tie them all together."

Sheila began tying knots. "I don't know what good it will do to have a rope. Who's going to pull us up?"

"Michael."

"I am?"

"Sure. Sheila can boost you up. You're light and you climb like a monkey."

"I'm scared!"

"We're all scared, Mikey. But you're the only one who can help us now. No one will be out there — they don't even know about this tunnel. There are bushes to grab onto when you reach the top. Just take the rope to the nearest strong tree, wrap it around and tie a good, tough knot. You can do that — I know you can."

"Okay," he said in a shaky voice.

"Ready," said Sheila. She had just enough room to crouch down. Michael climbed on her shoulders and she straightened her legs, pushing him up.

"I can't quite reach the top!"

"No problem," Sheila told him, grunting under his weight. "You're light as a feather." She put her hands under his feet, took a deep breath and pushed, grunting again with the effort. "Yes!" she said a moment later.

Clutching one end of the rope, Michael scrambled over the edge and disappeared. It was so quiet now that they could hear each other breathing. Katie wriggled forward until she could look up at the circle of night sky. It seemed like ages before a round shadow, the shape of a head, appeared there. Rusty shone his light up at Michael's grinning face, then Sheila tested the rope and climbed up.

Before Rusty climbed up, he handed his flashlight to Katie. She shone it on the floor, spotted her own flashlight and crouched to pick it up. Something else lay there on the dirt floor, something that sparkled in the flashlight's beam. She picked it up and held it between her fingers. A ring! A wide, gold ring inset with a square cut ruby.

"I'm sorry, Sir Charles," she said. "You might have made it out of here if you hadn't liked eating so much." Then she noticed Rusty's knapsack tucked neatly beside an arm bone. "Oh, Rusty." She shook her head.

She tossed the flashlights, cell phone, and ring in Rusty's knapsack and had just enough room to squeeze it over her shoulders and grab the rope. A small circle of black sky beckoned overhead, dusted with stars.

Once safely on the surface, Katie looked toward the

sea, where a full moon sprinkled its light over the dark water. She took a deep breath of fresh air and felt the earth beneath her feet — exactly where it belonged. She bent to give her brother a hug. "Michael, you're a hero!" she said. Then she pulled out Frank's cell phone and dialed 911.

• • • • • •

The four of them made their way through the bushes and stopped just above the tunnel. A large cabin cruiser was tied at the end of the wharf, its inboard engine running quietly, bubbling water out behind. The boat looked black from stem to stern.

Directly below, a wide ramp was set in place from the tunnel mouth to the wharf. The ramp was almost level now because the tide was unusually high. Set on the ramp, not far from the tunnel entrance, was that large, ugly sculpture Chuck had lugged outside just before the kids had made their escape. Voices came from inside the cave, the words unclear.

"Stay here," Katie whispered, and climbed down the bank. She crept as near as she dared to the tunnel mouth and listened.

"Almost got him." She recognized Chuck's deep voice. "A few more good pulls should do it!"

"Ahhh!" moaned Frank. He swore at his brother. "You're tearing all my skin off! You're doing it on purpose!"

"'Course I am! Would you rather we leave you here?"

"Quit bickering," Carlson told them angrily, as if they were little boys. "I need to think." There was a pause. "Anderson, I want you to take the gun and go upstairs to get those two cops. Frank's right. We need hostages."

"Can't, Chief," Anderson told him in a matter-of-fact voice.

"And just why not?" Carlson yelled.

"Frank's got the key in his pocket."

"Oh for … can't any of you do anything right?"

"If you want the key, why don't you help me pull him out of here?" Chuck grunted.

"Give me one of those legs!"

Katie clambered back up the bank to the sound of Frank's screams.

"Okay, we've got to move fast," she told the others. "Sheila and Rusty, here's what you do, and hurry, there's no time to lose." She quickly explained her plan, and they took off toward the house.

"Michael, come with me."

Katie and Michael scrambled down the bank as far as the ramp. Taking hold of the thick door to the tunnel, they slowly, quietly pushed it shut. Then they hurried to the far side of the sculpture and pushed. It wouldn't budge. They tried again, working together, straining with every bit of strength they had.

"It's no use," said Katie. "That thing is way too heavy for us."

"One thing I know is how to make things fall over,"

Michael told her. "Remember when I knocked over Mom's china cabinet?"

"Yes! Go for it, Mikey!"

Michael scrambled up to the very top of the sculpture. Then he leaned out as far as he could, waving one arm in the air. The sculpture wobbled but didn't fall. Katie moved between the sculpture and the tunnel door. She reached up. Michael stretched down and grabbed her hand. She pulled. The sculpture leaned toward the door, then started to fall. Katie yanked her brother out of the way just as the heavy sculpture toppled and crashed against the imitation-rock door. It didn't break but stuck there, on a perfect angle, wedging the door shut.

"Hey!" a voice yelled from inside. Someone pounded against the door, shouting and cursing. The door didn't move.

Katie turned to her brother and raised her hand. He jumped up, hit it and grinned.

"Let's go see how Sheila and Rusty are doing," she said. They heard the wail of approaching sirens as they ran around the house, up the steps and through the wide-open front door. They found Sheila and Rusty in the kitchen, sitting on the closed trapdoor.

"We couldn't find anything heavy to put on it," Sheila explained. "They've taken everything downstairs already. Come help."

Katie and Michael stepped onto the door, adding their weight. And not a moment too soon. There was a thump from below. Then a voice right beneath them that sounded like Anderson's said, "Hey, what's going on?"

They could feel the vibration as he pushed and then pounded against the door beneath them. "I can't get this stupid door open!" he yelled. "It's stuck."

"It can't possibly be stuck!" Carlson bellowed.

The sirens grew louder by the second. When they shut off, Katie knew they were close.

Anderson tried again, pounding desperately against the bottom of the trapdoor. "It is stuck, I tell you! I can't get it open."

"Hang on." Carlson sounded disgusted. "We've just got Frank out. What a mess! Chuck will be right there to help you."

... sixteen ...

Ancient Mystery

"Sheila, what on earth is going on here?"

All four jumped and looked up. Sheila's mom and another uniformed police officer stared down at them. Sheila quickly explained. Before she was finished, two more police officers joined them. They surrounded the trapdoor.

"All right, then," Ms. Walton said. "You can get off now. As soon as you do, I want you to run into the next room. Is that clear?"

Before they could move, there was a great, loud thump from below, and the trapdoor raised slightly. It settled back in place.

"It's stuck, all right," Chuck boomed. "Stand back."

Ms. Walton motioned for the kids to go, and they ran into the next room. They stopped and turned around in time to see the trapdoor explode out of the floor with a surprised Chuck Carlson right after it. He fell forward under the force of his blow, the upper half of his body sprawled on the kitchen floor.

"Get away from there, easy now," said a policeman, training a gun on him. Chuck pulled himself into the room.

Another policeman looked into the open hole. "You with the gun, hands above your head and get up here, now!" Anderson, white as a ghost, his hands shaking so hard he almost dropped the gun, stepped into the kitchen. The policeman took his gun.

From below they heard the sound of feet scrambling over loose rocks, heading for the tunnel.

"Don't worry, said Katie, grinning. "They won't get far."

· · · · · ·

Outside, standing in the light of Ms. Walton's police car, they watched the four men loaded into other cars and taken away. When Elaine Walton turned to her daughter, she transformed suddenly from a police officer into a mother.

Her face went weird. At first Katie thought Ms. Walton was angry, and she wondered suddenly if her own parents would be mad at her and Michael. Her brother would be in especially big trouble because he must have left home without telling anyone. Mom would never have let him come here on his own.

But looking more closely, Katie was not so sure Ms.

Walton was angry at all. She looked too busy being re-lieved and happy at the same time. She threw her arms around her daughter and hugged her so tight Katie thought Sheila would pass out.

Katie looked down at Michael, now clinging tightly to her hand, and hoped the same thing would happen with their parents.

As if he read her thoughts, Michael said, "Mom and Dad are gonna be mad." His voice was quivering.

"Why did you follow us, anyhow?"

He looked up. "I was scared."

"Scared? Of what?"

"I thought you would fall in the water again."

"Oh, Mikey," she said, bending to give him a quick hug. "You don't have to worry about me. I can take care of myself."

A car came rumbling down Rotten Road and skid-ded to a stop.

"Oh-oh," whispered Katie.

Katie's parents, followed closely by Rusty's mom and dad, all tumbled out and ran over. A minute later Katie was being hugged and squeezed until she was sure she had turned bright purple.

"Russell," said Rusty's mother, "will you ever stop getting into trouble?"

"He saved our lives!" Katie said. "He jumped back into that horrible tunnel to help, even though he was real scared." She punched him lightly on the shoulder. "Thanks, Russ."

He shrugged and looked embarrassed.

"So —" Katie turned to her parents "— does this mean we aren't in trouble?"

"Just wait," said their father.

"We'll talk tomorrow morning," added their mother. She turned to Rusty. "Your parents are coming over too."

"We'll be there," said Sheila's mother. "We need a plan to get these kids safely through the summer."

"No fair!" Katie protested. "We should be treated like heroes! We solved a crime that goes back over a hundred and forty years! The police never did find out who robbed MacDonald's Bank or where the money went! And we found Sir Charles Matthews too! He must have fallen into the escape tunnel and got stuck! Elizabeth said he was portly! And we know what happened to Elizabeth! And what about the art theft?"

Her dad seemed unimpressed. "Even heroes have to pay the price for their misdeeds," he said.

"Hey," Russ suggested, "do you think it would help if we go down to the beach and wash before we go home?"

For a few seconds everyone stared at him. Then Katie, Sheila and Rusty all started laughing. Michael looked totally bewildered.

The adults only shook their heads and wondered.

... Author's Note ...

Mystery from History is a work of fiction; the characters exist only in this story and in my imagination. Even so, Sheila is based on my very best friend during school days. I never could run as fast as her, jump as high as she could or skate as well — which was endlessly frustrating! Also, she had, and still has, the most wonderful freckles, which she always hated and I always envied.

The old mansion too is fictional. However, when I was about twelve years old, there was a huge old house on Victoria's waterfront. My friends and I were convinced it must be haunted. So one day I gathered all my courage and tiptoed up the stairs while my three fearless friends waited on their bikes, ready to take off at the first hint of danger.

To this day, I am convinced that when I peeked through the window, something moved inside the house. Naturally, I assumed it was some terrifying specter, either alive or dead. But I ran away so fast I will never know for sure.

Although my haunted house story ends there, for Katie and her friends it was just beginning. Katie is far braver than I ever was.

Historical references to conditions in the 1850s and 1860s are authentic. Those characters too, except for brief mentions of Governor Douglas and Dr. Helmcken, are entirely fictional. However, Victoria's MacDonald's Bank really was robbed and the culprits were never found, even though the police had their suspicions at the time.